LALA ROSA GIRLS

NAJOUA MARTIN

Lala Rosa Girls

Translated from the Dutch by Isa van Klaveren and Joni Zwart

Shabby Boat CM Productions

Original title *Meisjes van de Kapsalon* © 2014 *Najoua Bijjir*
Published in The Netherlands 2014

Copyright © 2021 by Najoua Martin
Copyright © 2021 Shabby Boat CM Productions, Rotterdam

English translation © 2021 by Isa van Klaveren and Joni Zwart

Cover photos: Winne Willems
Graphic design cover: Michiel Niesen
Graphic design interior: Michiel Niesen

ISBN 978 90 831728 9 7

'All that we see or seem
Is but a dream within a dream'
— Edgar Allan Poe

CONTENTS

For Oscar van Gelderen
who has been an inspiring mentor to me for the last 25 years

CHAPTER 1

F'dila

Real women smell of garlic

Is it the intimacy that takes Hatim back to his childhood or is it my smell? Is the secret of our attraction merely a scent? 'F'dila, the women in my village smell exactly like you,' Hatim says. In time, all female sweat will smell like sour Swiss cheese.

In our village in the countryside in the mountains of North Africa, we washed once a week. It was mostly on Sunday and I went to the bathhouse with the girls next-door, which was fun. The bath we took was so extensive that it took the rest of the afternoon to recover. They kept refilling the large tub with boiling water so the temperature was always nice. We sat on rickety wooden stools, splashing large amounts of water over our heads with a bucket. This ritual in itself took hours. The bathing was followed by a treatment with *sabon el beldi*, a natural soap made of olive pits that would purify the skin and open the pores. With a pumice stone we then scrubbed off the mix of butyric acid and dead skin cells, that had accumulated on our skin all week – I remember feeling layers of dead skin rolling off my body. After exfoliating, we washed and combed our hair with shampoo, a fine-tooth comb and lots of hot water. In our village, those nit combs pass for regular ones – because, really, you can't get all the muck out of your hair with a brush and a little shampoo, right? Once we had exfoliated the top layer of our skin and smoothed our hair, it was time for the *ghassoul*-mineral clay from the Atlas Mountains, applied as a mask on our hair and our skin. It made us feel even cleaner and we shone as if we'd dipped ourselves in olive oil. Finally, we washed our hair with shampoo again. The final phase was one last and symbolic round with the soap – this too took at least an hour.

It's all very different with those trollops these days. They shower each day, but never longer than three minutes. Imagine how those skin cells keep accumulating! They dye their hair yellow as saffron and cover themselves in clouds of perfume. Then you only have yourself to blame, I think, when your husband cheats on you and leaves you for a country girl like myself.

Shit-for-brains! Every single one of them. One day I will show them what I'm capable of. I am that poor village girl who will teach them a trick or two. They'll all be dead jealous, particularly all the people from my village. I will never forget how they were cheering when I left town! 'Village witch' they called me, and 'voodoo-terrorist'. I'll never be able to forget that. Once I have my papers, I'll build a proper life. I'll buy a luxurious apartment and drive around in the latest Mercedes S-Class. Boubker has promised me one, but first I have to learn how to drive. How hard can it be, when all you have to do is follow the road?

I'm wearing my linen skirt as it's a special occasion and I want to make a good impression on Hatim. It's a very wide thing, which could easily be turned into a tent. The pockets are large, so I can put the blow-drier in them as well as the other things a hairdresser needs.

As of today, I shall be a real hairdresser! I'm quite proud

of it. I've been dreaming of this since I was a young girl and moved away from our mountain village, to live with my aunt in the big city. As I had no further education than primary school, I worked as a housekeeper for various people. The jobs gave me a lot of freedom at a young age, because I was making my own money.

One thing I have always known for sure, though: one day I will be either a hairdresser or a wedding stylist. Cutting and dyeing hair or doing make-up for brides – that will be my future. This is my first day as a hairdresser. Honestly, how hard can it be, when all you have to do is cut?

It was easy to find a job in the big city. I was relieved to become the live-in housemaid with a family and leave my aunt. She was meddlesome and reported everything I did to my family and neighbors in the village.

My room, a sort of attic, was above the storage room and was nicely decorated. There was a bed, a television, a wardrobe with mirrored doors and a sink. The floor was covered with a floral carpet. Much better than the cold, hard floors at my aunt's place and the dry sheepskin I slept on as my aunt kept the luxurious bed to herself. The couple I worked for encouraged me to take as much from the pantry as I liked, but I was obliged to eat in the kitchen – it had to be clear that I was not part of the family. I was also expected not to interfere with the children. That was not part of my duties. And so, there was hardly any contact with the children. I did not mind at all. I take an interest in a great many things, but not in children.

I could use the shower whenever I wanted. A huge luxury; hot water came pouring out. I was not used to that. At home we had to heat the water on a gas burner or, worse, a pile of burning branches or charcoal. The people I worked for were wealthy. They had a beautiful villa. Both worked as professors at the University. I thought they were posh, just like their friends and relatives visiting them. Their children were so well-behaved that I often wondered if they were entirely sane. I had not seen anything like it in my life. The children in our village clambered on roofs, had mud smudges on their cheeks and pebbles in their hair. Sometimes I believed the children of these professors were possessed by ghosts, so I just steered clear of them as much as I could.

People visiting the professors were always dressed in *djellabas* made of the finest silk. They wore matching high heels, custom made, and carried the most gorgeous handbags. Even the women who wore a *hijab*, like I do, all looked extremely beautiful. Deep in my heart, I hated them. Who did they think they were? I had anything but warm feelings for Mrs Professor too – I detested her. The bitch probably felt the same about me. Each morning, she sat in front of the mirror in her bedroom to do up her hair and put on a lot of make-up. She was just a teacher, but she thought she was Her Majesty the queen. She used a lot of expensive perfume. Such a pungent smell! For no good reason I slipped the bottle of Givenchy in my apron pocket one day. I took it with me to the Netherlands – as a keepsake you might say – and to use it on very special occasions, such as this one.

She bossed me around, that hag. Each morning she dictated my duties for the day. What was she thinking? That I was one of her students? I had to sweep, scrub the walls and mop the floors. The mistress wanted a spotless house each and every day. 'The neighbors might come for tea later.' I can still hear her say it. I had to do the laundry, shop at the grocery store and pre-cut the vegetables so everything was ready when she came home and started cooking. That woman would make the weirdest dishes! I often didn't like half of them. As for her husband… I mean: what man wants to eat stuffed roulade in slices, as if he were in a restaurant? Tajine with dates and crepes… Ridiculous! If he'd been my husband, he would have been served proper food; split peas with lots of olive oil! And for dessert, I would have made fat-filled, home-baked oil bread and a glass of tea so sickly-sweet the enamel would pop off his teeth. *That's* what men like!

Every day, to keep my culinary skills up to standard, I watched a fancy-schmancy cooking program on television. I scribbled each recipe in the notebook I had kept from primary school. Did that lipstick cow really think she was the only one who knew how to make crepes? I would trump her with my truffle couscous. She was teaching at university, but I would show her who, between the two of us, was the professor in the kitchen.

I hated her so much that I fantasized about hurting her. I would go to the healer. He would give me something terrible to stir in her food, so first she would shut up and then she would slowly crumble like old concrete. Who would be in charge of this place then?

I regularly practiced black magic. I tied knots in cloth and blew on them; a ritual to get Mrs Professor stuck in her life. I had learned this in my village, where I secretly watched a woman who was very skilled at it. One day I caught her feeding her husband donkey ears to dumb him down – mercilessly cut from an animal in the village.

Before long, I began to suspect that my victim, Mrs Professor, was carrying a very strong anti-voodoo amulet. Obviously, the frequent blow attempts and double knots were not working. After some deliberation, I decided to give in to my true feelings and take it one step further. On my next day off, I scooped one of the mistress' sanitary napkins out of the trash can on the patio. The bin had been broiling in the blistering sun all morning. I really had to dig deep into the grunge – it was disgusting, what a mess, I was in it up to my elbows – but the hard work paid off in the end. That same afternoon I took the bloodied napkin to the healer. After a very long wait (there were at least twenty people before me) I was allowed to enter.

I explained what I wanted and then the doctor mixed the blood from the sanitary napkin in an amulet with human bone and lots of other things. At least, that was what he claimed. I had heard that this doctor had undisputed superpowers. My girlfriends said he could turn water into ice. If I'd have had the money, I would have asked him to show his skill to me right then and there.

The doctor told me to bury the amulet in a child's grave. That was a problem; the nearest cemetery was miles away from my workplace. I would never be able to go there unnoticed. I had another few days off two weeks from now, but that would be far too long of a wait. I decided to bury the amulet at night. Not long before I had met a tramp in the city center. He was a simpleton, one of those bums who dream of one day owning a villa with a pool and an Audi, but now spend their entire day smoking, sniffing glue and squandering the little money they have. I asked him to accompany me to the cemetery for a small fee.

In the dead of night, while everyone was fast asleep, I left the house, armed with a flashlight. There was no sign of life anywhere – apart from a pair of eyes suddenly lighting up. I was scared stiff and thought I had run into a ghost, but quickly discovered that it was just a cat.

The light of my flashlight was reflected in the eyes of the beast that followed me to the cemetery.

I met the bum on the outskirts of town. He threw stones at the cat.

'Stop it,' I whispered. 'What if it's a djinn… You don't want to get into a fight with ghosts, do you?' He looked at me incredulously and then said 'There is no bigger ghost than you.'

The journey seemed endless. In the dark, I tripped over stones and nearly sprained my ankle. If only my assistant had a car, but he was too big a failure for that. Moreover, he seemed too tired to exchange a single word with me.

Once we arrived at the cemetery, we quickly found a child's grave. It had a small tombstone with a number engraved on it. The tidiness and the fresh plants showed someone had visited the grave quite recently. I told my companion to dig a hole – I myself preferred to keep my nails clean.

'F'dila, this is really a big sin!' He tried to protest, but when I reminded him of his fee he started digging with his bare hands, still grumbling that voodoo is a ticket straight to hell. Well, that was one thing I could do without.

'Shut up,' I said, 'it'll be light soon!' Idiot. I have been wearing a hijab, long skirts covering my ankles and a very neat apron since I was twelve. I can hardly become more pious, can I?

The visit to the healer had cost a lot of my savings – money that was actually reserved for my mother who had stayed behind in our village and had become severely ill, but my expenses and great efforts began to pay off after just a few days.

One morning not long after the night at the cemetery, I noticed that Mrs Professor was not commanding me in her usual way. On the contrary, I found her in bed, racked with pain! She lay there like a sick rabbit, with barely anything left of her radiance and intellectual respectability. She complained about stitches in her abdomen and cramps which, according to her, were worse than contractions. She was groaning with pain. I was almost tempted to put a sock in her mouth. I can't stand people wailing like that – even if they are sick.

In the following days, the mistress vomited a lot — so much so it seemed her organs would shoot out of her throat. Perhaps this inconvenience was caused by the powder the doctor had given me to put in her food. It was made from dried hyena brains, among other things.

Weeks later, the pain in her stomach still hadn't gone. The mistress had stopped having her period. She lost weight. After eight weeks, no more was left of her left but a skeleton covered with skin. From the side she looked like the broom handle I swept the floors with each day. Scary blisters appeared on her lips. There was no other way to put it; that doctor had done an excellent job.

And Mr Professor? He drove the Mrs Professor everywhere to find a doctor who could cure her. The entire family even went to Paris for a few days to visit one there, but it was all in vain. No doctor knew how to treat her. No one had an explanation for her symptoms, not one examination led to anything. Mrs Professor had called in sick at university. She no longer put up her hair and she no longer sprayed clouds of perfume on her neck. Instead, she turned into something resembling a dry piece of fruit, shriveling and moldering more each day – even hungry vermin would not touch her.

In my carefully detailed plans, there was one thing I hadn't taken into account; now that the mistress was at home, she needed care, she could no longer cook, no longer mind the children and she no longer took them to the day care center.

The new situation brought about an enormous amount of work; I was busier than ever! Normally all my work was done by seven o'clock. I was only expected to wash the evening meal dishes late at night. In between there was plenty of time to go into town with my friends – in the summer we dressed up, hoping to catch ourselves an emigrant on a family visit. From the first day my mistress got sick, I worked overtime – she did pay me for it, but I hated all the extra work.

The tension in the villa rose day by day. The children were bored and noisy and the mistress gave everyone sleepless nights with her moaning. To make her suffer a little more I told her, when she was sitting on the edge of her bed, that one of the maids across the street had mentioned that the husband of a sick woman nearby was planning to divorce his wife. He thought she was too ill and was therefore looking for a new, young woman. 'But fortunately, things between you and your husband are fine, aren't they?' I asked with a vicious little smile at the end of my story.

Every day I brought her some 'news' that I had thought up the night before. She bought it all! I loved the effect of my gossip: it was like hot oil on a fire. The arguments between Mr and Mrs Professor became more and more intense and the lamentations grew longer. While I peeled the potatoes, the mistress sat at my kitchen table crying. I feigned genuine interest, always curious about all the ins and outs, and the next day I would come up with a rumor that would increase her anxiety even more. How is it possible that someone responding this naively to my tricks can be a professor? I outsmarted those supposedly intelligent people on all fronts!

One day I decided that the time had come to make my move. 'This is the moment,' I told myself in the mirror. After all, I knew how to seduce and satisfy a man… That's one thing you learn growing up in a village. The strangest things happened when girls and women went to the well on the outskirts of town late in the evening or at night. It was dark, you saw no one and no one saw you. In the day time everyone pretended nothing ever happened.

I was not troubled by guilt towards my victim. Mrs Professor was highly educated and made enough money to support two entire villages. She didn't need a husband at all. I, however, *did* – and I would be best off with a rich man. Age and looks did not matter to me; I was and still am willing to marry any man with enough money to make my dreams come true. And if I tire of him, we'll just get a divorce, right? At least then I'll have a claim to half of his property. Mr Professor had an attractive fortune and for that reason alone was a man after my heart. The villa was an excellent home for me. Sometimes I completely lost myself in fantasies of redecorating it after our wedding party. I had already drawn up a list of wedding guests and had the best wedding stylist in mind to do my clothes and my hair. We would do the whole wedding all over again in my old village with the same stylist and wedding band. After the party, Mr Professor and I would drive back to my villa in his Mercedes. The only one keeping my fantasy from becoming real was Mrs Professor. And she, as I was pleased to establish, was now very seriously ill indeed.

I did feel sorry for the mister sometimes. He had to live with an unhealthy woman. A woman who has something wrong with her is at the bottom of the social ladder. As are women who cannot have children. They are compared to fruit trees that bear no fruit. Such trees, as far as I'm concerned, can be cut down without mercy.

I thought Mr Professor was a poor thing. That man deserved a woman, a real woman. One like me, really. I don't mean to brag, but in many respects I am preferable to other women. I wear a hijab, I often sit with a rosary in my hand, I am very good at boiling potatoes and I knead oil bread like no other. I can slaughter a chicken or rabbit if I have to and if they offer me a cow and a slaughter knife, I will not hesitate to cut that animal's throat too. In fact, I am willing to quarter it and turn it into the most delicious dishes on the very same day. A woman who is a professor is not a real woman, is she? Real women smell of butyric acid, onions and garlic.

One night I made my move. I dressed in see-through pajamas – with nothing underneath. The transparency, as I'd checked in the mirror, was perfect. I had not washed, I smelled of fresh sweat and I was wearing my most beautiful headscarf.

It went exactly as planned – as if I was acting in a play I had directed myself. I had just entered the kitchen when the mister walked in – as he often did in the evening, to pour himself a soda. In my pajamas I leaned forward in a seductive pose, pretending to scrub a stain off the floor. Gosh, I was good. I really enjoyed playing this game.

I heard him gasp. He held his breath in his throat, the way you hold a fly in your fist. I looked up, smiled modestly and bashfully played with my cleaning cloth. Yes, I have another specialty: like no other I have the gift to let my eyes tell men what I want them to do. I got up, looked him in the eye and lured him into the pantry. I had barely started massaging his member when Mr Professor came. I was not really impressed by what he produced. Were those children actually his? The Professor walked out of the pantry with his head hanging low and I left for my room, intensely happy with my first victory.

My triumph, however, was short-lived. The next day the mistress got a visit from friends who persuaded her to see a medicine man. 'This is taking way too long. This smells fishy,' I heard them crow. It had gradually become a habit that I listened in on conversations between the mistress and her friends, just as I always searched their bags. One always had chewing gum and a comb in her bag, and never more money than a hundred Dirham. How can someone be so posh and still only carry a hundred? Shortly afterwards my mistress, the bitch, visited a medicine man. My chances of marrying her wealthy husband were gone in an instant. All up in smoke! Within a week she had completely recovered. Her husband, whom I had stood in the pantry with just one week before, personally threw me out of the house. I shouted to the mistress that her husband had 'deflowered me!', but that cry for help was ridiculed. No one believed me. And when I scratched up my face with my fingernails in pure despair and went to report abuse at the nearest police station, my case was treated with a lot of suspicion. Mr and Mrs Professor also came to tell their story and they brought witnesses. This was enough reason for the police not to register my report and instead show me the door with a warning. I briefly considered suing Mr Professor for rape, but quickly dismissed that idea as nonsensical.

In the following weeks, I spent day and night cursing the fact that I had failed to get Mr Professor to knock me up. It all turned out so different than I had scripted. I was convinced that in that case the Professor would have left his wife for a future with me. My big wedding in my village with a Mercedes and a wedding stylist… I had come so close to my goal, but all my dreams were destroyed in one fell swoop.

And now I'm here… In the Netherlands, in Rotterdam, with no papers. I am not sure what is worse; that I am illegal here or that I still don't own a villa and Mercedes?

'Every day is a new opportunity,' I tell myself as I look into the mirror. But this time it must not go wrong. This time I will take it slowly. First, I want to make Hatim completely mine and then you'll see that he will marry me. And the wedding in my village will take place after all, and after the party, they will all be waving at me, the happy bride. There will be no more gossiping about me. Married means married. And no one will have anything to say about me ever again. Everyone will respect me. I will finally have a husband. I will finally be a person with papers.

With great care, I wrap my headscarf tightly around my head; a little too tight, but it does look nicer. I smooth my white blouse with my tense fingers. It has an old-fashioned French collar and fits well on my worn-out skirt. I pick up my apron from the oak table Boubker bought from our Indonesian neighbor. Hatim and I are meeting in a cafe, but I decide to wear my apron anyway. It's not just any old apron, but one made of fine cotton. The border is decorated with embroidered orange and green buttercups. I slip my wallet into the front pocket, and also the fake ID card that Boubker, the sweetheart, has arranged for me via his friend Jaap. I'm not too fond of Jaap: his breath smells disgusting because of all the coffee he drinks and all the cigarettes he smokes. Actually, Boubker himself smells like a moldy ashtray.

I spray a dash of Givenchy on my headscarf, put on my coat, grab my bag and leave the house.

Outside on the street, Boubker is waiting for me with a burning cigarette between his lips. 'Hurry up or you will be late,' he calls impatiently as soon as he sees me. I quickly wrap my coat around me, tugging at the belt around my waist until it's really tight. Boubker must not see me wearing the apron over my clothes. If he gets wind of that, he will instantly send me back upstairs and order me to take it off immediately. It annoys him when I wear an apron. 'What idiot wears an apron when they go out?' He says. 'If you are so intent on wearing it, do so inside. Then at least you create the *impression* of doing some chores.'

Boubker and I are not married, but we do live like a married couple. He firmly refuses to arrange papers for me. I don't know why, but he once vowed never to do that for anyone and sticks to that decision. It's fine by me. Boubker is courteous. When I get in his car, he holds the door for me and when we sit down to eat, he slides the chair under my buttocks. As long as I have a roof over my head and a guy who feeds, dresses and protects me, I am more than pleased. Especially now that I'm getting a job as a hairdresser and my childhood dreams are coming true. How can I complain?

I can barely keep up with Boubker's rushed steps. What a strange man he is, you can never be sure whether he's cheerful or grumpy. With him, this can change per minute, so I'm often walking on egg shells.

We hurry across the Erasmus Bridge. There is a strong wind and we are walking straight against it.

As long as I can keep up with Boubker, he won't turn around and grumble at me for walking too slowly. And he won't see the apron. Poor Boubker; he has no idea why I'm wearing that thing. And he never will.

'It's over there, on that side.' Boubker shows me the way with an outstretched arm. We have to pass the traffic light and then turn right.

After passing a large intersection, we enter a narrow street where there's roadwork. Why did we not come by car? Boubker can be so weird sometimes.

We arrive at the cafe-restaurant where I'm meeting Hatim. You must go through a revolving door to enter. That's quite shabby, I think. I much prefer electric sliding doors, they are classier than one of these stiff revolving doors that is far too narrow. We walk past the reception. The heat from the kitchen hits us in the face.

'Have you been struck by lightning, is that it?' Boubker freezes right in the middle of the cafe-restaurant and starts growling at me without any mercy. He has seen my apron. Now what? I can hardly tell him that I want to impress Hatim.

'You ah-calf,' Boubker says in slang. 'Ah-you could have come rolling out of the mountains like this. The stones still stick to your feet. Ah-calf... Do you not see... Do you not see that this is too moronic for words? This is a place where decent people come. Old Dutch ladies come here, business-men... Ah-are you really this stupid?'

I think that's enough. 'Boubker,' I say, 'shut up and stay out of women's business.'

'Alright, but if you go around looking this ridiculous, I don't want to be seen with you. And certainly not in Hotel New York. If my colleagues would see me with you like this...' and he mutters on. His grumbling does not go unnoticed. Astonished and angry looks come our way. Imagine: a burly, stern looking Moroccan man walking in front of his veiled wife, stamping his feet while she meekly follows him. The picture perfectly corresponds with the idea Dutch people have of Moroccans. If only they knew what it's really like! Although... those who value prejudices will continue to believe in them. Muslim women do nothing but slave away in the kitchen and obediently follow their husbands. No truth can beat that, these people here are so naive. Losers...

I let my head sink a little deeper and pull up my shoulders. I wrap my arms around myself like a frightened bird and from underneath my eyebrows, as suppressed as possible, I look at all the Dutch grannies and businessmen sitting here. My fingers disappear – oh, what a sorry sight this must be – in the pockets of my apron. After all, you never know if there is a rich Dutch man here who wants to free me from my oppressed state. The one condition is that he's willing to arrange papers for me and marry me in my old village – *and* we are most definitely not going on a honeymoon by plane, but by car. After all, you cannot park an airplane at the front door for everyone to see. That apron is fantastic and I am brilliant. I should get an Oscar for best actress! I will blow all those actresses over, with their toothpick bodies and overpriced dresses. Not bad for a farm girl in an apron!

Boubker is impatiently tapping the table with a coaster. The waiter is ignoring us, not for the first time. I saw his gaze slide over my apron. If he could, he would have ripped it off me and pushed it into Boubker's face. And he would have shouted: 'This is not how we treat our women in the Netherlands, you hear me!' Oh well, all men are losers. All women too, actually. And it doesn't matter where they're from. I rise above them all… I rise above everyone.

What is keeping Hatim? I'm starting to get thirsty and the waiter just won't come. Boubker has given up, he will not be served by this waiter. For several minutes Boubker has been ignoring everything that is going on around him. He seems crushed that I'm wearing an apron to this meeting. There are always just two options with Boubker. Either he gives in, or he loses it.

Boubker was once a wealthy man. Unfortunately I didn't know him at the time. He ran a fiberglass company, had his own staff and made a lot of money with this business.

He emigrated to the Netherlands with his parents when he was seven and his life proceeded like any other from there. He worked hard, smoked, got into running and he went out with friends once every two weeks. Apparently he never had any problems. No one really knows why one day he simply lost it. Some people thought it was because of politics, which he followed closely via radio and television. He still does. I often tell him it's much better to watch Moroccan television via the satellite dish. 'It will cheer you up.' I myself follow a great soap opera and I also love the live glamor concerts from Lebanon. No bullshit about migrants, immigrants and descendants of immigrants on Moroccan television. Not that it affects me, I couldn't care less. But that's not the case with Boubker. He feels hurt by the way he's being treated in the society that he is part of. 'It's a waste of time,' I keep telling him, 'to worry about that. They don't want you if your hair is black and that will never change.' Jaap, Boubker's friend, thinks it's 'very upsetting' when I say that. I ignore him, because Jaap knows perfectly well that I'm right: they don't want you if your hair is black.

The story goes that one day Boubker withdrew all his money from the bank, climbed on the roof of an office in the city center and scattered hundreds of banknotes in the air. It was a madhouse. People are said to have parked their cars in the middle of the road where they got out to gather the money. Young people did not know what was happening to them. Boubker never saw one cent of his money again. On the wall of that office building he chalked in large white letters: 'It's done now, so leave me alone.' At least that's what they say.

I don't know why Boubker stays with me or why he has allowed me into his life in the first place. If I'm being honest, I have to admit that he's far too good to me. See, he could easily have hooked one of those pretty chicks with saffron hair and lots of perfume. One who can't cook, works in an office and drives a small Mazda. He probably lacks courage and zest for life: he's still on medication and regularly sees a doctor. He goes to work every day and the rest of the time he just sees me and Jaap. He doesn't give a shit about anything else.

From the window here in Hotel New York, you can see the swirling water of the Maas river. Further down I see Hatim come in via the side entrance. When he casually sways the swing door open, he brings in a strong gust of wind. Hatim greets us briefly and sits down at our table. A few minutes later, he and Boubker – who have not met each other before – are in deep conversation. Hatim has not even bothered to look at me. Tsk-tsk. As if I don't exist.

Only yesterday I sent Hatim a picture of my naked bosom, but now I wonder if it impressed him at all. Instead of just thanking me with a wink, he argues with the waiter, because he is not being served quickly enough.

'Or do you not serve Moroccans? In that case I'll just go somewhere else.'

'No sir. As you can see, it's very busy,' the waiter explains. He takes a gasp of air and is about to add something else when Hatim beats him to it.

'Well, pour me something strong then. Whatever you have. And what do *you* want?', he says, turning to me. For a moment, we lock eyes. There's a naughty twinkling in his. So he *is* impressed by my message.

'Fanta Orange,' I answer with a smile.

Hatim's eyes glide over my apron like a wet sponge. They take in my entire body.

'Make it an orange soda… and a small ice cream for the lady,' he tells the waiter.

'A small ice cream?' the waiter asks, a little surprised. 'Alright, I have noted one scoop of ice cream.'

I feel embarrassed, but Boubker is completely unaware.

Then the job interview starts.

'So, you will come and work in my hair salon?' Hatim asks.

'If you want me to, yes, please.' I can barely speak the words and I turn my face away. I play my role of humble servant girl perfectly.

'Alright. I'll show you the salon later. Ladies only, you know that, don't you?' He glances sideways at Boubker. 'No men allowed. So you'll have to introduce yourself.' Again he turns to Boubker. 'What is your plan?' he asks.

'You go, my shift starts soon,' he replies softly. He has left his tea untouched.

'When she's done at the hair salon, she will call me and I'll take her back home. Or one of the ladies,' Hatim says. It seems intended as a reassurance. I say I could take the tram back home.

'No,' says Hatim. 'You are picked up and brought home. When we are given something to look after, we handle it with care.' He winks at Boubker, but he does not respond.

After Hatim has paid, I walk with him to the parking lot where the wind hits us in the face. Hatim, unlike Boubker, doesn't seem uncomfortable about my apron. I like it when a man stands by his woman and is not obsessed with what people may or may not think of her. For the first time in my life I step into Hatim's sports car. The upholstery shines beautifully and inside is a wonderful smell of vanilla. Would all expensive cars be like this? Oh, I can't wait to get my driver's license. And this Hatim, what an incredibly nice man he is.

'Hang on a second,' Hatim shouts, pressing his mobile phone firmly to his ear. 'Souad… Souad…' He taps his screen again. When the other side answers, he yells: 'Souad! Are you at work? Good, listen! I'm coming by with a new hairdresser. She's coming to work in the salon with you! Do you hear me? Can you turn the music down!'

A pause. Then he starts again, quieter this time. 'Yes, she's coming to work in the salon. Make sure you treat her well. She's my cousin and she's going through a rough time. Do you hear me Souad? No, you will be treating her *well*.'

I push back comfortably against the seat. The view across the water is actually beautiful here… I can be pleased. The first step has been taken. Onward to step two: making sure, in the most subtle way, that Hatim's wife, owner of the salon, disappears from the scene. Then Hatim will arrange my papers. He will have to divorce his wife first and put the salon Lala Rosa in my name. Then I will sell the business and with the proceeds I shall buy the latest Mercedes as well as a villa in my village and I will celebrate with the biggest ever wedding… A wedding my fellow villagers will never forget. And then we'll see who still dares to call me 'village witch'. Tomorrow, first thing in the morning, I will start looking for a healer, who is just as good as the one I visited before. The sorcerer that will make my dreams come true.

'Nice app message yesterday.' Hatim says it with a grin. Then he starts to drive slowly across the parking lot. The car is of such high quality that you don't even feel the uncomfortable bumps underneath your butt… It's as if we're driving over butter.

'I am so embarrassed,' I lie. 'That nude photo was meant for Boubker. Really, I don't know what to say.'

'Why?' Hatim asks with surprise, 'Do send me such pictures more often, beautiful.'

Hatim reduces speed and parks his car on the side of the road. 'You know F'dila,' he says, 'I want to tell you something.' He suddenly sounds very serious. 'You remind me of my childhood, my mother and my sisters when I was young… Your modesty, your bashfulness, your beautiful apron. It all makes me so emotional. You really move me with your appearance. I don't know anyone like you.' He gently caresses my cheek. 'You are so pure.'

I smile shyly. Oh, Hatim, if only you knew. 'Tell me when you want me…'

Hatim's finger firmly brushes my lips and disappears into my mouth.

'Fasten your seat belt,' he orders.

When we hit the road at full speed, I am certain. Today a new time has come. As of today anything is possible.

CHAPTER 2

Souad

Men and money

'Souad, you've really gone too far this time,' I mutter to myself. Tottering tipsily on my glittering heels I make my way through the hall of *Tapis Rouge*. I wonder if I can still get a cab at this time of night to take me from the club to the station. The train from Brussels to Rotterdam takes forever, ugh. I should've just set up a date, or asked someone for a ride before I walked out of the club, but I'm way too good for that. Men should chase after me and not the other way around, you know.

Loud music is blasting from the club as I pour the contents of my green cocktail glass into the big succulent in the empty cloakroom. I take the tasteless gum out of my mouth and with nothing else at hand stick it on one of the plant's leaves. Cocktails and chewed out Bubblicious are definitely *not* a tasty combination. Licking the syrupy remains of booze out of my cocktail glass I realize I have to be careful now, or I might actually be tipsy when I get to Lala Rosa... I can already hear Layla's sermon on *haram-this* and *haram-that*. That's the last thing I need right now. I'll just take her to the club one day, that intellectual smurf posing as plain Jane. As if! I'll fill her up with Bacardi-coke without her even noticing. Hopefully that will stop her nagging about what's right and what's wrong. What's 'right' is barely discussed anyway; at Lala Rosa it's mainly about what's wrong, *haram*, bad. I actually wonder what that Layla has been up to herself? Nobody's perfect, you know. Anyone who says they are is a lying bastard. She'll probably loosen up and start talking after a few drinks…

'Hey, you! Lady! Where do you think you're going? You still have to pay, remember?' As I turn around and realize what's going on, I quickly get into character. Pretending to be completely wasted, I giggle loudly, waving my fingers in the air like some high-class conductor. 'Stay here!' the owner of the club gruffly pulls me by the straps of my tiger print top. Seriously, if this thing rips that nutcase doesn't know what's coming for him! Does he even know what I paid for it?! Three Hundred Fifty euros! For this piece of cloth! The things I had to go through to get the money… I even smooched that pudgy Najib… ugh!

'You are not leaving until you pay the bill!' the man roars. What? So now his radar eyes noticed me sneaking out of his club without paying?

'Darling!' I exclaim like a first-class slut, dropping my sweaty armpits on his shoulder. As I embrace him, I find my balance on his thin neck – some men have a very broad body, but a tiny head and a thin neck. Deflated balloon heads I call them. Their opposites, the blown-up balloon heads, are men with a small body and a very large head.

The man protests and tries to wiggle himself free from my grasp. I say: 'you can… You can al, al, alw…'

'The bitch is wasted! I swear, she's not leaving, not before she's paid her bill! It's been so many times now, I've lost count! I won't do it anymore! Do you hear me! I won't do it anymore!

Those bitches will ruin me this way!' the man bellows, repeatedly trying to remove himself from my grip. His scrawny body seems unable to wriggle free from my sturdy embrace. The crackerhead is so scrawny, that I can fold him up and pin him to the wall just like that.

'You can...' I pinch the man's cheeks until they come together. He makes me think of the red sea bass I saw in the fish shop's window this afternoon. His eyes are starting to bulge now and steam is very nearly coming out of his ears.

'You can always come by for a perm or a bikini wax with me.' I make it up on the spot, enhancing the impression that I'm completely wasted, and the drunk one never pays the bill. Further exaggerating, I drop myself on the floor with a loud crash. The pain in my hips and back is intense. My performance is so elaborate I should get a friggin' Oscar for it, but I'd do anything to avoid paying that awful bill.

'You're gonna pay or I'm calling the cops!' the owner yells, saliva spewing all over the place. Oops, I was expecting a little more pity from Mister *Tapis Rouge,* pity for a girl in need like me... He's not really calling the Brussels police department, is he?

'How much was it?' I hear someone say in the background. What a relief. I was getting the slight impression that I was in dead trouble this time. I've got a feeling it's anything but fun to spend the night in some greasy cell here in Belgium.

'Well,' the owner begins to sum up, 'for the lady and her friends who left earlier: two VIP tables, the extra cocktails... hang on, I'll get the check.' The nutcase has seriously written everything down. This guy makes tons of money on those VIP tables every weekend and he's still a cheap bastard when it comes to a couple of drinks.

'No need.' Rasheed stops him right there and reaches for his wallet. 'Here's three hundred. Is that enough?' The owner takes a surly look at the money. 'Right, right, here's four,' Rasheed hands him the notes with a sigh.

Me and my party girls always 'take care' of the check like this. We all take turns to deal with our expenses at the end of the night. Last week it was Fenna's turn: she pretended to be dead drunk at some fancy restaurant and managed to avoid paying. Us party girls, Fenna, Dunya, Joyce and I always create a lucky escape. And in *Tapis Rouge* there's always some good Samaritan with a lot of money. A Samaritan like Rasheed, in this case.

One time Dunya was busted, however, when a disco owner kept her locked in the staffroom until the police came to get her. She spent that night in custody, and was given a fine and some community service, as this wasn't her first time. It was so embarrassing when I saw her grubbing the city gardens. I walked on quickly, pretending not to see her, and she in turn pretended to not see me either. Luckily it turned out well this time… Imagine me grubbing around like some drudge. As if!

'Alright then,' Mister *Tapis Rouge* says, immediately slipping the money into the inside pocket of his tailor-made suit. Then he disappears behind the big heavy doors of the club. 'Great,' Rasheed says, but I'm not entirely sure what he means by this. In an attempt to pick me up off the floor, Rasheed breaks out into a sweat. 'God, you're heavy, no wonder with that huge ass of yours…' I struggle not to burst into laughter, but I can't afford to get out of character now and be presented with the check after all. Intertwined, we stagger across the parking lot, where Rasheed's BMW is waiting. His heavenly perfume covers me like a seductive cloak. Men with money just love tiger print, you know.

On the drive from Brussels to Rotterdam, I pretend to fall asleep with a raging headache and ignore Rasheed completely. When, after an hour, we pull over to get gas, I drowsily order a large Latte Macchiato and a double Snickers. I have to start toning down this fake drunkenness before we arrive at Lala Rosa and my shift at the hair salon begins.

I'm kicking off my sobriety tour as soon as Rasheed hands me the large latte. He has already stirred the sugar into it, the sweetheart. 'Here, drink up.' 'Thanks,' I say and take a big bite out of the candy bar.

As we approach Dordrecht, I ask Rasheed to pull over really quick. On the side of the A16 I make some very convincing puking sounds. Luckily, from where he's sitting, he can't really see me behind the car. I stick my chewed out Bubblicious on his number plate and help myself to a new piece of gum.

'Bueeehhh!' I roar as loud as I can, and again 'Eeub-beeuughhh!'

'Are you okay?' Rasheed asks me, leaning out of his window. Thankfully, he still can't see anything of my fake vomiting session. 'Yeah, I am, now that all the alcohol has come out… It's the first time I've ever had any, so that's one thing I'll never do again,' I make it up on the spot as I walk back to the passenger's seat.

'You know what,' he says, very seriously, 'good girls don't drink. And you seem like a very good girl to me. You're beautiful, you have a nice figure, you look good, what man doesn't wanna be with you?'

'Thank you, baby,' I say and place a kiss on Rasheed's large forehead with a multitude of wrinkles and a receding hairline. I try to look him straight in the face, but Rasheed's eyes are hard to find between the bloated bags hanging under his eyes like a permanent pile of misery. Even if you'd rub ten tubes of hemorrhoid cream on them you wouldn't be able to smooth them out.

'Don't I get a kiss?' Rasheed asks me breathlessly from his

seat, pouting his sticky, child-like lips – the fact that I just vomited all over the place doesn't seem to bother him. This Rasheed does have some serious dough, you know, so I say: 'alright then,' and press my plump lips on his. I had them botoxed just a month ago, so the idea that Rasheed is kissing plastic instead of me is somewhat comforting. In my mind I imagine I'm looking at something else to distance myself completely from Rasheed and his ugly face, but the amazing perfume he covered himself with and his money are making it all OK. Besides, I've become an expert in disconnecting. I can actually handle any man, because it's like I can unplug myself whenever I want. 'Hhrrr…emmhmmhh…' Rasheed is not even trying to hide his pleasure, it's disgusting. When I include the check he paid for me before and his amazing car everything is totally worth it.

'Babe, I have to go to work soon', I tell Rasheed, looking at the clock on his dashboard. It's eight fifteen already, ugh!'
    'Are you going to work like this? This drunk?'
    'Well, I have to, babe, I don't have any money,' I say, instantly filling my head with ideas. 'You know, I saw a pair of boots at Shoebaloo, and I really want to buy them. But as I said, I don't have any money.'
    'How much are those boots?' Rasheed asks with the right amount of interest as he's filtering into the highway traffic. Properly indicating direction, he immediately steps on it. With a car like this everyone gets priority, and that's exactly the way the world works. When you have money, you go first. When you don't, you'll be ditched.
    'Fifteen hundred euros.'
    'You know what,' Rasheed says, 'I'll get them for you. See it as an early birthday present.' His hand then disappears between my thighs, but as soon as he approaches my panties, I

jam his greasy fingers with my upper legs. I'm that slut who hasn't slept with anyone yet, you know. I'm still a virgin and that's how I wish to keep it. Until I've found my 'real' man, that is, and he is not just anyone I happen to pick up at the club.

Rasheed pulls away his hand and lets it rest on my lap. He's a pretty good guy, you know. He's not one of those drugs dealers or shady people. He's a successful certified public accountant who works for a big firm… Or does that automatically define someone as shady? Whatever. He's probably still single as he's always coming to the club to feel 'good'. Most men hang out there to feel like a 'man' among all those bitches lurking after them.

'Don't you work for that shady guy… what's his name again?' Rasheed says, interrupting my contemplations. 'You mean Hatim?'

'Yeah, that one… I get the feeling he's the sketchy type,' Rasheed says.

'I don't know. I go to work and I get my pay, that's all I have to do with him,' I tell Rasheed. In the meantime, I place his hand on the brake and snatch my gray cardigan and tiger print leggings out of my bag. Then I clumsily remove my lace tiger print skirt and wriggle myself into the tight leggings. As soon as I undo my seat belt the car starts beeping.

'Does he even own the place?' Rasheed asks me suspiciously. 'Yes, he owns the place.' Annoyed, I wrap my cardigan around me and roll up the sleeves. I hate it when people are being so vague! Drowsily, I examine myself in the mirror. I rub some camouflage on my forehead and cheeks. Overall, I still look pretty good, even though I haven't slept for the past twenty-four hours. Which is just great by the way, when you still have a full day ahead of you. Oh, and then there's the new hairdresser starting today. That what's-her-face… 'F'dila.'

'What?' Rasheed asks me.

'Oh, nothing, I was just talking to myself.'

My hangover is suddenly nowhere to be found. I hope I don't smell of alcohol?

'Oops,' inhaling my own breath, I realize it's nothing but tequila and Bubblicious, so I spray a small cloud of Chanel into my mouth. Without him noticing, I stick my gum underneath Rasheed's car seat.

Rasheed honks loudly as I stick the rusty key into Lala Rosa's door. He then blows me a kiss, like a real Romeo. 'Byeeee,' I wave cheerfully. Bye loser whom I just relieved of two thousand euros. With a sense of accomplishment, I caress my black Prada bag with my acrylic nails. As I open the door, I instantly notice the lights are on.

'Well, well… sir,' I say, as I hang my cardigan on the coat rack. What's that asshole doing here this early in the morning?

'Good morning, beautiful. Where have you been all night?' Hatim asks me.

'Nowhere, and you? Were you with your wife and two children?' I emphasize the last four words. His wife Baktha who has never shown her face around here. When do we get to see her? I know how Hatim thinks about us, you know. His eyes betray him, that's Hatim. If you know him long enough, you can tell anything by the look in his eyes.

'What's that?' Hatim suddenly starts pulling funny faces. 'What's that you say?'

I curl my lips and walk towards the small kitchen to get myself a coffee. Hatim follows me closely. 'Where's that cousin of yours?' I try asking him, but Hatim doesn't answer me.

Men are like toddlers, you know. First, they whine about a

red lollipop, and once they have it, they'll start whining for a blue one. You'd think Hatim would be busy enough with his wife Baktha and all those girls from the club he spends his nights with. Just the other night I saw him with some blonde from Dutch television. Before long he will start believing he's a celebrity himself.

'What would your wife think if she'd see you here like this?' I threaten with a wink.

'Enough about my wife,' Hatim says, dismissing the subject. He then comes dangerously close. At first, I hold my breath and brace myself, but soon I start giggling. 'Ha, ha, ha!' Tickling in the neck, that's something I've never been able to resist. I instantly fall for the fooling around. Hatim's breath rolls pleasantly across my neck.

'Do you like that, baby?' Hatim blows on my bare shoulder with his plump lips. 'Ha, ha... cut it out, loser!' I slap him off me, as I would do with a fly. But Hatim just doesn't know when to stop, so I ruthlessly slam him with my massive behind. 'Please!' He lands on the coffee machine, which is standing on some rickety table. That thing will fall apart someday, you know. They should've just placed the coffee machine on the kitchen countertop or on the floor.

'Kiss me,' Hatim invites me. It's gross. 'Ugh, well alright... I've seen these boots at Shoebaloo, but I don't have the money to buy them,' I say, lost to shame.

'How much are they?' Hatim asks, like the crackerhead he is, already checking his pockets for his wallet.

One by one Dijana plucks the ladies' eyebrows like chickens and Layla is blow-drying like crazy. With an extremely heavy blow-drier she's attacking Jasmina's thick frizzy hair. There is just no getting used to those stinky blow-drying fumes. That burnt smell always dominates the salon. It literally smells like burnt scalp. Sweat is dripping from Layla's temples like water from a tap, but Jasmina doesn't seem to care. As long as your hair's nice, I guess. Our customers are convinced your hair should be as straight as possible and preferably as unbendable as a wooden cheese board. Some of our customers even go the extra mile and iron their hair at home. Just like that, with a hot iron on the ironing board.

F'dila is waiting on the doorstep. In her long raincoat she looks around helplessly. Hatim can't be serious, coming up with a farm girl like this. It is obvious F'dila is overwhelmed by the wedding-dance-music and the blasting of blow-dryers, shaking your brain like a guzzling V6. I myself have noticed my hearing has gotten worse since I started at Lala Rosa.

'Who's that?' my customer Tee asks me from the hairdresser's chair. 'Our Holy Hairdresser,' I roll my eyes towards the ceiling, 'you know, the type that's been flown in straight off the donkey's back.'

'Well, come in already!' I say impatiently to F'dila, who is staring at the floor in embarrassment. Why does she keep standing there? It's always crazy busy in the salon and we can definitely use an extra pair of hands. Then she opens her long old-fashioned raincoat revealing the lamest apron. 'Who's that, Mary Poppins?' one of the customers yells at me. 'Shhh,' I gesture towards the rickety waiting area table. She's Hatim's cousin, we're not allowed to fire her, not under any circumstance. So, bullying her out of here is also out of the question.

'Is she *actually* wearing an apron?' Layla asks no one in particular. 'Ha, ha, she can't be serious!' 'That's typical Hatim, showing up here with some country-bumpkin,' I add. 'You think she's any good?' Layla asks me, dividing Jasmina's hair with hair clips so she can straighten it with the blow-dryer. Even before I can answer her, I'm interrupted by the woman in the green djellaba sipping coffee in the waiting area: 'Well, it was about time you girls hired a cleaner. All that rubbish on the floor, and that horrendous, filthy bathroom! Simply sickening!' 'Ah-go read a magazine,' I tell Green Djellaba.

'So, is she any good?' Layla asks again, and she pauses briefly to wipe the sweat off her forehead. 'Well, if you ask me, she probably bought her scissors at the supermarket,' I say, pulling a precision comb out of my tiger print leggings to divide Tee's bushy curls.

'Shut up, F'dila might hear us!' Layla waves her blow-dryer around. 'Whatever,' I say, and get some hair clips from the dressing table to pin Tee's thick head of hair. I don't even understand why Tee has her hair blown dry here, because she always wears a hijab. 'Oh, and Hatim told me we can't fire her, not under any circumstance,' I tell my co-workers, 'because she's his cousin,' I say as I give them a wink.

'You can work over there.' Dijana directs F'dila to the spot on the other side. F'dila instantly walks over to the empty working station.

'I was wondering, are you the manager? Or Dijana?' Tee asks as she turns to face me. She reminds me of a wild tiger now that her bushy hair is completely loose.

'What do you mean?' I answer curtly.

'Of course, it's not you,' Tee says, looking relieved.

'What do you mean? You don't think I'm fit for the job?!'

'Ah-that's not what I meant!' Tee bursts out, but before she has a chance to finish her sentence, I interrupt her. 'Ah-turn around, girl! How can I blow-dry your hair like this,' I say, annoyed, smacking the blow-dryer softly on the crown of her head.

'Ouch!'

'Sorry.'

'So, who *is* the manager here, anyway?' Tee asks in another attempt to have her question answered. Meanwhile she's trying to untangle herself from my grip and wipes the hair out of her face, which is hanging in front of her eyes like a curtain. 'I really don't know,' I answer, making it really clear this time. 'Maybe I am the manager,' I consider on the spot. 'I open the salon every morning and always have minor details to discuss, that's what a manager does, right?'

'You're right. I think you are the manager,' Tee decides.

'Hatim's the manager,' Layla suddenly joins the conversation. She then clicks off her blow-dryer and, standing in front of the mirror, starts waving around her peroxide blonde hair, which has been blown-dry straight as an arrow. Her shallow appearance hides the fact that the silly bitch is actually highly educated. She always wears skinny jeans, sneakers and pink lipstick.

'Right, yes… Hatim is the manager,' I suddenly realize. 'But Hatim is the owner, right? Now I'm confused.' I ruffle Tee's rough hair as I try to think. Oh well, I come here every day to do my work and I get paid every month. Even if some clown were the manager, I wouldn't give a shit.

'What about his wife?' Tee asks us, looking at herself in the mirror. Her chin is covered with scars from popping her zits. 'You should stop fidgeting with your face the whole time!' I smack my blow-dryer on her shoulder.

'I can't help it! You want me to leave them there, then?!'

'Rub your face with Azulene paste!' The old lady in the green djellaba advises from the waiting area. She's still sipping her coffee.

The girls who come to Lala Rosa always want to know the ins and outs on everything. And by that, I mean *everything*.

'Hatim owns the place, but the business is in the name of his wife Baktha,' Layla says, staring blankly into the mirror, after which she turns on the blow-dryer again.

I don't know what's gotten into Layla lately... Something's going on, but I can't figure out what exactly. She's been acting cold, distant, and she looks quite pale. 'The lady seems to be annoyed,' Tee whispers. 'Who, Layla? No way, she's always that chippy,' I explain to Tee. But Layla does seem to be more absent-minded than normal, she doesn't seem to be present at all.

'Ah-come on, stick to your blow-drying.' Layla is waving her slim finger at me, but the mirror gives away her desperate gaze. What's going on with that skinny carrot? And why have we never seen Hatim's wife around here? Well, if you ask me, I don't have to see that woman at all anyway. Especially as I'm always fooling around with her husband here, and getting paid a great deal for it, too! But the fact this business is in her name does put the whole situation in a different perspective... Oh well, I get paid every month, so what do I care.

While the customers are sharing recipes for zits, blackheads and spots, which they picked up from a cooking show on TV, my thoughts wander off to Layla, my colleague who'll soon graduate from law school. Blow-drying is not easy today. My muscles are still killing me after my performance at Tapis Rouge... What's going on with Layla? Maybe she's been so absent because of her studies, she might be struggling with finishing her thesis. That must be it. That bitch just can't graduate. Our lady studying 'law'. The word itself makes me sick. I just can't get over the fact my fellow hairdresser will have a university degree soon, and I don't have anything, ugh!

Life can be a hard pill to swallow sometimes, and so unfairly divided! You know what kind of dough a lawyer rakes in every month? I wouldn't even need those men from the club, I could buy everything myself!

'Ouch!' Tee screams suddenly. I hadn't noticed I dropped the blow-dryer that hard on her head. 'Oh, sorry,' I say, soothingly petting her hair.

I then throw the blow-dryer in Tee's lap without a warning to get myself a fresh piece of gum.

'Would you like some coffee?' Esmaa asks. She's the journalist who always wears red turtlenecks with holes in them.

'Love some!' I roar, knowing full well that coffee doesn't mix with Bubblicious. For a second my thoughts go back to the green cocktail of last night and the scrap with the owner of Club *Tapis Rouge.*

'Would you like me to make some coffee?' F'dila asks, smiling.

'Fine by me,' the journalist says and returns to the rickety table. She immediately resumes her conversation with the woman in the green djellaba.

'The new girls always make the coffee here,' I say jokingly. Layla doesn't even notice. Instead she mechanically continues blow-drying Jasmina's hair while staring at some spot on the floor like she's mesmerized.

After some time F'dila walks by carrying a tray of coffee, and she asks Selma to take a place at her new working station. Then, all of a sudden, the women at the rickety table start gossiping. For a week now, the entire salon has been obsessing about this Mona I never heard of.

I watch Selma take a seat in F'dila's chair while she continues gossiping with the waiting area table via the mirror.

Is the Apron Lady any good actually? I don't trust her; I don't trust that F'dila at all. When it comes to women, my intuition never fails me. Besides, Hatim never even said any-thing about that cousin of his. And why is Lala Rosa in the name of his wife?

The same gossip has been repeated ten times this week, still I can't help but listen. 'Mona has been drugged by her family in law and stuffed in a burlap sack. They then threw her in the trunk of their car and sent her back to the village where she's from.'

'Oh,' I say, frowning. I trade my precision comb for my Jag-uar scissors. When I'm listening to gossip, I always love to cut. 'I'll just do your split ends,' I whisper in Tee's ear.

'*Wili, Wili,* do you hear that?' I turn towards the rickety table where a handful of customers are hanging on Green Djellaba's every word.

'In a burlap sack,' I hear Dijana mutter. 'Those people up here!' she says, tapping her sweaty temples with her index finger.

'When they arrived in Mona's village, they took her passport and her papers from her,' Green Djellaba continues, waving her hands around. 'Seriously? That's nasty,' I answer sharply.

In reality I have a slightly different opinion on the situation. Which is: 'Good for you, you hypocrite farm girl!' It's goody-goody's like her that make girls like me look like sluts, while they themselves pull the dirtiest tricks.

I leave Tee's hair for what it is, grab my own locks and cut some split ends.

'And didn't her ex abandon their son, too? I can't believe how a man can leave his own child!' I exclaim as I smack my hand onto the back of Tee's head.

'*Wili, Wili,* are you abusing me or doing my hair?'

'Oh, I'm sorry' I answer, putting the Jaguar scissors back into my leggings as I pick up the blow-dryer from her lap to resume the blow-drying session.

'Souad, golden blonde!' Dijana suddenly roars in my direction.

'Alright!' I say, and sigh deeply. Everyone always comes to me when it comes to mixing dye. Oh well, that's just how it is… I'm simply indispensable here. People need me, that means I must be the manager then. Perhaps it's time I start negotiating with Hatim. A manager's position should come with a manager's pay, right? Maybe I'll have some of those special business cards made. I can picture them already…

Souad
Manager Lala Rosa
Follow us on Instagram

You know, just to show off in the club among those rivalling tarts. A manager is a kind of owner of the place after all. So maybe I'll just make it:

Souad
CEO Lala Rosa
Follow us on Instagram

That sounds much better already. Daydreaming about my soon-to-be status I stir the bowl of golden blonde I'm preparing for Dijana in the small kitchen. 'Golden blonde, right?' I yell from the kitchen back into the salon. I don't know why, but I sometimes seem to suffer some kind of amnesia. Maybe it's because I regularly pull all-nighters.
    'Golden blonde, yesss. And hurry up!'

As I stir my brush in the bowl with the hair dye, I suddenly hear loud cries piercing right through the music. '*Wili, wili, wili!*'

I pass the rickety waiting area table and watch Selma banging her fists on her own head.

'What have you done?!' Selma ruthlessly pulls the hair out of her head, like a stressed parrot plucking his own feathers. 'You bitch! I don't have any eyebrows left! I have no eyebrows! I have no eyebrows!'

The color in the container looks beautifully smooth. It gives me a real sense of accomplishment when the colors have mixed perfectly. 'Here you go,' I hand the dye to Dijana, who takes the container and puts it into her customer's lap without thinking. Luckily the customer catches it right on time, otherwise all that work would have been for nothing.

Dijana makes several attempts to calm down the situation, but she can't get a word in.

'Listen, don't worry about it,' Dijana says, sweating. 'I'll make everything alright.' Dijana bangs on her own chest. 'Do you hear me?' But Selma can't utter a word of sense. Instead she desperately looks at herself in the mirror. Her eyebrows belong to the past now.

'See, I told you,' I sigh, noisily chewing my gum. 'She probably bought her scissors at the supermarket.'

CHAPTER 3

Layla

Lady law

'Ouch!' I scream out in pain. I quickly turn the blustering blow-dryer off. My finger is turning red. It's throbbing and will blister soon.

'Just my luck, ugh…'

'Layla, are you okay?' Olfa says as she turns to face me.

'What?' I ask, staring at Olfa's outfit with astonishment. Seriously, our customers show up in the weirdest creations.

'Are you okay?' Olfa says, perplexed.

'Oh, yeah. I think so…' I answer, but I'm distracted by the nude leggings Olfa is wearing. They are decorated with lively ink figures, making it seem as if Olfa frolics around the streets of Rotterdam-West with bare tattooed legs.

'You seem absent-minded lately,' Olfa mentions casually as she takes a packet of cigarettes out of her bag.

'Sorry, you're not allowed to smoke in here.'

'Oh, well, rules exist to be broken.' Olfa clearly doesn't care and lights up a cigarette.

While Olfa is smoking her cigarette, I switch the fuming blow-dryer back on. Of course I'm absent-minded. What do you expect with all those tax bills for the hair salon, hurled into my mailbox like frisbees? How am I gonna explain all this to my dad? Inadvertently, a tear drops from my eye. I catch it with the sleeve of my T-shirt just in time.

What am I to do now? I pour my despair into blow-drying Olfa's crunchy hair, but somehow the roller brush just keeps getting stuck.

'You're gonna have to take home a bottle of Kérastase, your hair is dry as straw. How do you want it done, anyway?' I say, as I rummage my fingers through Olfa's hair. 'Very smooth and straight', she says.

I had no other choice but to break up with Hatim…

'Ouch!' My middle finger burns like hell. I put it in my mouth, so I can soften the pain with a lot of saliva. It's not even the blow-dryer I keep burning my fingers on, it's that smoldering hair, glowing like hot coals. I really don't understand why people set their hair on fire with a glowing blow-dryer, or worse; when they set to work with an iron at home!

'You must be careful not to burn your fingers. Happens to me all the time when I'm straightening my hair,' Olfa informs me. Self-assured, she then crosses her tattoo-like legs and swaps the home-magazine for the worn-out glamour magazine Grazia, which is on my shelf. The magazine, sealed and delivered brand new only yesterday, looks as if stray cats have used it as a litter tray.

Olfa seems amused about an article on a Dutch socialite. It's the talk of the salon. Some famous football player is single again. One visit to Lala Rosa and his bachelor-status is history. You know what it is with this type of women? They actually succeed in seducing such men. Somehow these women always have their way. For a second my eyes wander to the trophies Olfa managed to gather. The very expensive bag, the diamond rings and those revealing leggings. I wonder if I'll ever get rid of my single-status? The first and last relationship I've ever had was with Hatim, the jerk.

'Hey, are you blow-drying the hair sideways?' Olfa says, heavily agitated. She makes frantic attempts to untie herself from my blow-drying grip, but the roller brush is intertwined with her locks. I'm having a hard time balancing the heavy blow-dryer, so I involuntarily let it rest on her crown.

'*Wili, Wili!*' she screams, as she gets into a fight with the roller brush. Then she mercilessly pulls the strain of hair and the roller brush straight out of her head. Ouch, that's gotta hurt. She furiously plucks the hair out of the brush with her fingernails.

'I always blow-dry it like that,' I sigh. The gigantic blow-dryer is now dangling below my waist. It doesn't matter what position I take; the thing always causes muscle-aches. My back and shoulders have really been killing me lately. It's not tennis-elbow I suffer from, but blow-dry-elbow.

'Dijana always blow-dries it straight and she presses the blow-dryer really tight to my hair, so you get actual fumes escaping. Not like those wobbly hands of yours!' Olfa says, angry as hell.

'What, do you want me to burn it?'

'I want you to blow-dry it, like Dijana does,' Olfa orders, curtly.

'Where is Dijana...' She looks around questioningly.

'She never works on Wednesdays. You know I'm always alone on Wednesday mornings, right?' I say as I try my best to swallow my annoyance. Types like Olfa are not to mess with, you know. They're often involved with the 'wrong crowd' and I'll be hanged if I know the things they do to get their money.

'Everyone knows the way I work, okay?' I clarify to Olfa.

'Would you please carry on blow-drying now?' Olfa carelessly throws the magazine on the shelf, which causes a few things to fall off, including a used cotton swab. Not long now before I smack her with that blow-dryer.

The front door opens with a bang. 'Olfa, is there a problem?' Hatim's voice always crashes down on me. I drop my shoulders despondently, the device still dangling next to my legs. How can it be that you first love somebody so much, and then all of sudden that love turns into disdain and contempt?

Lately it's as if Hatim only comes here to torment me, or is he here because of Olfa? I wouldn't be surprised, those two half-wits.

'Why, is there something wrong?' I show Hatim my prettiest smile, even if it's an impossible task. I am now determined to apply my new strategy; honey catches more flies than vinegar.

'Hatim,' I say sweetly, 'can we have a chat in a minute?' I give him a wink. It's the same wink he once fell for. The wink that helped me pay for my studies. Without Hatim's sponsoring and generous pay checks I would have never been able to afford a university degree. I've had to pay the price, though… What if my parents find out? What if the debt collector turns up at my doorstep? I'll be ruined! Or worse; what if I then get an audit, I'll never be able to open my own legal practice! But there's still hope… Hatim might cooperate, or I might even be able to exploit the whole situation and make him pay for the entire practice, that's still another option.

Hatim pretends I'm not even there. 'What's wrong, babe?' he asks Olfa, glancing into the mirror and neatly folding the high collar of his shirt. He's not an ugly guy, on the contrary. Hatim is a very handsome man, but it's that 'creepy' side of him that makes him unattractive. 'Nice little hairdresser you got here,' the bitch says. 'Nice little hairdresser' 'Ah-get lost!' I want to spit at her, but of course I don't.

'What, is she not doing her work properly?' Hatim says, annoyed. My wanting to 'get out' of our secret arrangement did not go down very well with Hatim, that's obvious. On top of that he is showing psychopathic behavior. His mood can flip, out of the blue, from furious to cheerful and the other way around. I don't know how he manages to produce a heavy dose of endorphins one moment, only to supply himself with a shot of progesterone the other.

'I'm just blow-drying,' I say desperately, visualizing a massive jar of honey with my future legal practice floating in it. 'It's normal to tilt the blow-dryer a little... Here, see,' I demonstrate on the spot, 'it keeps you from burning the hair. If I don't, I'll burn her hair. Then it breaks and it's done, and before you know it, she'll be bald,' I explain to Hatim.

'Ah-just blow-dry it as the customer wishes,' Hatim waves his hands, clearly annoyed. 'The customer is always right, remember? Besides, with that much hair I doubt if she'll ever go bald. Honestly, I've never seen anyone with hair as thick and firm as this.' Hatim is now inspecting Olfa's hair like he's the expert. 'You know what, why don't you blow-dry it some more, it might become soft and smooth again.'

Olfa giggles and I don't know why. Is she really that stupid?

'Okay, have it your way,' I grumble. Then I shove the blow-dryer to its very hottest. Now the device doesn't roar anymore, it rages. A hurricane would pale in comparison! I put 'the beast' on maximum heat and press it to Olfa's head like a bazooka without thinking. She screams and pulls herself away in full force. 'Hold up, sit still, don't move,' now it's my turn to hand out the orders.

Her cries of pain escape her throat in squeaks. Almost instantly a big cloud of smog lifts from her head. It stinks like crazy... The entire salon now smells of burnt hair instead of hairspray. The smoke penetrates my throat and even Hatim is gagging and covers his mouth with his hand. 'Something like this?' I ask loudly, looking into the mirror. Olfa is now twisting her fuchsia colored lips, as if she's unable to move her jaws. Even her mascara is starting to run. But she keeps herself together and raises both thumbs with a cramped smile.

What Hatim is up to behind me, I'm not sure. I can just feel him ferreting out the place; behind the counter, in the jewelry cabinet and in all the workstations. But nosing around the stack of letters from the debt collector, I don't think so! What if the debt collector shows up at my parents' house... Seriously, if my dad finds out he'll kill me!

I violently scrape the blazing hair dryer over the rigid ink-black hair, pulling the rolling brush as if my life depends on it. 'Oof!' I wipe a drop of sweat from my forehead. My muscles are getting sore by now. I breathe a sigh of relief when my phone rings. Without thinking, I drop the hot hair dryer into Olfa's lap and rush towards my shoulder bag. I first have to bend past Hatim, who is reading the paper in a swivel chair. He throws me a sharp look, and I give him one right back, asshole!

'You smell,' Hatim then says, indifferently and straightforward.

What's his problem? He doesn't say it teasingly, nor smiling or beaming, but he's dead serious. Blunt, hard, rude, cold.

'I don't smell at all!'

'Yes, you do. I can smell you from here.'

All I can smell are those disgusting burnt hair fumes. As discreetly as possible I sniff the synthetic shirt I bought at the market only a week ago... Shit, I look around in embarrassment. 'Can I speak to you in private later?' I ask him gravely.

'I'm busy,' Hatim says indifferently.

'Hatim, I have to talk to you later,' I say, and I take a step closer. 'I want out.'

'You're not getting out, you're staying!' Hatim says, his eagle eyes piercing right through me.

'Haven't you seen those envelopes?' I roar, 'The taxes have not been paid yet!'

'Ah-get lost!' Hatim starts again, 'You go do your blow-drying… I can do without the headache your bullshit is causing me!'

There's a knot in my stomach and I'm holding my breath. Breathe in, breathe out, I calm myself. I take a big gulp of air. The smell of burnt hair is nauseating. I can hardly breathe and cover my mouth with my hands. I must leave this place, run… Get out of this salon, I can't take it anymore! Without thinking, I move towards the front door, in the mirror I catch a glimpse of Olfa and Hatim fooling around. How could he after all the good times we had!

The street looks bleak and deserted, there's nothing to see but some passing cars. I step outside, into the cold and fresh breeze; my hair is dancing in all directions. What if the debt collector comes knocking on my door? What do I do then? A tear rolls over my face and I'm too late to catch it. Damn, my phone's ringing again…

'Yes, hello?' I say with a sob as I silently swallow the lump in my throat. I can barely hear myself speak with this loud wind. 'Hello?!' I press my other ear shut in an attempt to be able to listen.

'Hey darling, it's me.'

'Who's this?' I ask.

'Duh, it's Souad, *wili wili*, what's with you? Are you alright? You sound weird.'

'I'm outside and the wind… I can barely hear you… where are you?'

'Oh, you know…' Souad tells me, giggling, 'I'm here at the School of Management.'

'Excuse me?!'

There's a silence.

'I assume you're not planning on taking up some economic studies, or an MBA? May I ask what exactly you're doing at the School of Management?' The chaos that was messing with my head a minute ago, is suddenly gone with the wind.

'I'm here to pick you up,' Souad answers breezily.

'But you know I always work on Wednesday mornings, don't you?' I ask anything but kindly.

'You have a class at university in the afternoon, right? So I thought; I'll just pick you up from school,' she adds, sheepishly.

'You're picking me up from school?'

'Yes, and then we'll go shopping together.'

'But, duh; I'm at Lala Rosa every Wednesday morning, so what are you doing at the School of Management? You know I study law! That's in a completely different school building!' I'm suddenly ambushed by a splitting headache.

See, I should have never told Souad that I study law, let alone enlighten her about the existence of the School of Management where lots of businessmen follow special courses for top executives.

'Stop whining already… By the way, I've met this really nice guy here, he's a bit old, but he has a car with a built-in navigation system. In the windshield of all places! Do you hear me? In the windshield of his car! He's going to show me all the gadgets later, wanna come girl?'

'Souad, please don't do anything silly… I go to school there…' I utter in slight panic. What if it's a prominent professor, or worse: a lawyer from a renowned law practice. That Souad is going to put my reputation at stake! I really hope she's not wearing tiger print. One way or another… Souad is always wearing tiger print! That's what gives me a headache!

'Come on, don't worry…' Souad says, chewing her gum as she starts fading out. I hate it when she does that, starting a conversation with someone else in the middle of a phone call. It doesn't get trashier than this! I want to turn off my phone, but can't resist following the conversation with this flashy man and his built-in navigation shit.

'Ma girlfriend is gonna come and see what's up in a sec,' I can still hear her say. Why is she talking so boorish? At the School of Management of all places, I wish the ground would open up and swallow me.

'Souad! Souad!

Souad, can you hear me?'

'Yes, darling, I can hear you, I was having a conversation. You know?' she asks me, loudly chewing her notorious pink bubblegum, 'that man introduced himself to me… do you know some guy called Schmeegle?'

I can picture her already. Souad, dressed in tiger print, chewing her gum and smugly filing her nails in the fancy lounge of the School of Management, giggling and flirting with some guy called Schmeegle.

'Souad, I gotta go now.'

—

CHAPTER 4

F'dila

My kind of guy

'Alright then, F'dila, see you Friday.'

'May God protect you, I cannot express my gratitude,' I tell the doctor. Then I hang up and place my mobile phone on top of the wooden dresser in the hallway, next to the pink perfume box. Thankfully, the healer has his practice close to where we live. It's at one of the central docks south of the river, close to the café where Boubker and I met Hatim the other day. I quickly resume my beautification – Hatim can be here any moment. He's a real gentleman, picking me up at home in the morning and taking me back from Lala Rosa late in the afternoon. Really, Hatim is my kind of guy, I sigh… He has everything I ever dreamt of: a beautiful car, money and a business. I have finally found my man.

The doctor can see me this Friday already. I must be there before dawn. He stressed I absolutely have to be on time. I will go to his practice to engage in all kinds of unholy rituals. He'll call upon spirits to get all I need – to make my dreams come true.

In front of the mirror, I spray a misty cloud of perfume on my cream-colored hijab. Then I place the elegant bottle back into its pink box. I have to be there before 5:15 am. That means I will leave home at 4:30 am to go to the practice. The healer also instructed me to bring some of Hatim's semen. 'Then your loved one will be clenched in your fists forever,' he assured me in his leaden voice. Meanwhile, my mind is racing, plagued by a myriad of questions. How do I get semen from Hatim before next Friday? There is only one way...

I sigh deeply and inhale the fresh and floral perfume. Simply delicious. I check myself in the mirror, pleased with what I see, and open the drawer of our wooden dresser. There lies the spherical bottle of perfume I took from Mrs Professor. I decide to put the pink Chanel perfume next to the Givenchy... See, I simply couldn't resist yesterday when I saw the Chanel perfume shining in Souad's bag at Lala Rosa. At one point no one in the salon was watching, they were all too busy with Selma's plucked eyebrows. So, I took my chance... In a flash I swiped the perfume box out of Souad's bag and slipped it into my apron.

My fingertips lovingly caress the box Chance by Chanel and the round bottle of Givenchy. As if they are my two biggest trophies.

What I have done to Mrs Professor will pale in comparison with what I intend to do to Souad. The whore. As if I didn't notice Hatim's eyes rolling across that camel ass. Souad the monster has thighs the size of bouncy castles and a butt you could fit an entire amusement park on. Sometimes I wonder how many men have been riding that ass.

I see my reflection and frown. My blouse is really a bit too short for the mesmerizing zebra print pants I'm wearing. As I look in the mirror, I notice that my bottom is actually flat and triangular. The wide skirts I always wear never reveal such things. I also don't know what to make of the pants. Actually, they are too wide to pass for leggings and there's something pajama-like about them. I found these cheap pants at Primark yesterday afternoon as I was strolling through the shopping street near Lala Rosa. Dijana had given me half a day off after the epilation drama with Selma. 'Perhaps is better you come tomorrow,' the Eastern European had said to me. I did not object. I picked up my coat from the rack, greeted everyone and browsed the shops until Hatim picked me up from work again.

The socks with white fringes that I also found at Primark, certainly contrast nicely with my black pumps. I never wear heels, because that is an art in itself. I open the drawer of the wooden dresser again. I decide to hide the crumpled shred of paper with the number of the healer at the docks underneath the Chanel box. Boubker doesn't make a habit of searching cupboards. Even if you would hide a lover in them, he wouldn't notice a thing. Boubker is as unrefined as a cow and has the energy of a salt-bag. I cannot wait for Hatim to rescue me from this dump and provide me with a better life, a better life than this. Would this sorcerer be able to fix this for me? So Hatim will marry me with no further delay? After all, things went horribly wrong with the healer back home… All my plans with Mr Professor and then his wife, the witch, scrambling back on her feet, against all odds. My plan must not fail this time.

I was given the doctor's number by an old woman I met in the supermarket recently. You see, there is no such thing as coincidence. These things happen to me all the time. When there is something I need or have set my mind on, I always get what I want. Because I also have a magic gift, one that healers often have too… I know how to make things go my way. If only I knew how to take it from there, I wouldn't need that damn sorcerer at all. Then I would have taken care of my voodoo business myself.

The old woman I met in the supermarket seemed lost. I

asked her what was wrong and she told me she'd been spending the *entire* afternoon trying to find matches.

'Dearie, I do not speak the Dutch language,' the woman said desperately. She struck me as a little senile too. First, I wanted to walk on, but then I realized this woman might be of use to me in some way. 'Just a minute,' I said to the woman and I asked the first shop attendant I could find: 'Ah-lady, where do you keep those fire things?'

'Fire things?' the young blonde asked.

'Well, yes,' I said urgently. 'The fire things to make fire.'

'Make fire?' the young lady took a few frightened steps back.

'Ah-for cooking, right?'

'Oh, you mean a lighter.'

'Yes, I mean that… But then the wooden sticks.'

A few aisles further the old woman pressed her lips on the back of my hand. She asked who I was and if I was married yet. 'If I had a son, I would have asked for your hand right now,' the woman said, in a most friendly manner.

If only she had a son, a very wealthy son who would make all my dreams come true. Then I would have accepted her proposal immediately. Then I wouldn't have to bend over backwards to get what I wanted. I sighed away the thought and told her a story I made up on the spot. 'My sisters and I, there are seven of us. None of us is married. It's always the same,' I was fighting false tears. 'We're always approached by men asking for our hand. But when the moment comes, it all falls through,' and although my eyes were dry as dust, I blinked a tear out of my eye to reinforce my words. 'My mother has become so desperate… Seven daughters and not one who has been able to build a normal life.'

'Oh dearie, a beautiful young lady like you. You wear your hijab, an apron and a decent skirt… Any mother sees her ideal daughter-in-law in you.' The woman, holding the box of matches in her hand, hesitated briefly. 'Do you know what I think?', she then added, 'they must have used witchcraft against you, magic to block your fortune. If I were you, I would do something about it.' The woman narrowed her eyes.

'If only I could do something, but how?' I played ignorant.

'Visit a medicine man,' the woman said as she pressed a pointy finger in my shoulder, leaving it all bruised. 'You and those sisters of yours have to do something, because this just isn't right…'

I sighed deeply and said: 'I don't even know where to find one.'

'I know a really good one, he has a practice at the docks. He's one of those healers who can turn a glass of water into ice right in front of your eyes,' the woman said excitedly.

'But isn't visiting a medicine man haram?' I said, raising my eyebrows.

'Of course it is, but when in need… You are going to see the medicine man to help yourself… Even though it is a sin, if you know what I mean. Some people call this politics', and the woman gave an affirmative wink. A second later she pulled her mobile phone from the pockets of her djellaba with her sausage like fingers. She deftly pushed the buttons of the flashy device, something she was much better at than buying a box of matches in the local supermarket.

I pull up my striped zebra pants, which are too large really, and smooth out my blouse. I grab my pastel colored apron from the oak table and quickly put it on. I breathe in deeply, inhaling the smells of Boubker's sleep and cigarettes. I pick up the house keys from the dresser in the hallway and walk outside, wondering if the healer at the docks will be as skilled as the one back home. He knew exactly how to turn hyena brains into a dangerous magic powder. What he did to Mrs

Professor was quite something. In any case, I must and I will clear any obstacles out of the way.

Obstacles such as Souad. And I need to get hold of Hatim's semen before Friday.

'Well, well,' I hear Jaap say, as I leave our apartment building. He glances suspiciously at the zebra pants and the short blouse I'm wearing. 'Is Boubker at home?' Jaap asks. Why is he acting so stupid and why does he keep staring at my blouse and zebra leggings? 'No, why?' I answer him, annoyed. 'And where are we going today?' inquires the imbecile who spends his entire day smoking roll-ups and waiting for Boubker to come home from work. Although that dickhead Jaap is unemployed, his fingers are always grimy and stained with motor oil. 'Ah-none of your business,' I wave my hands. 'Easy...' Jaap grumbles as he puts another filthy roll-up in his mouth. 'Tell Boubker I'll drop by tonight.'

'Ah-Jaap, I have to work, you tell Boubker yourself! Don't you get it? I have to work!' I angrily slam the door shut. Suddenly I am standing outside in the cold. A cool gust of wind passes through my zebra pants and even my underwear. If I stay in this cold any longer, I'm sure to get a bladder infection.

Not much later Hatim's shiny sports car drives into the street. First, I turn around, to be sure Jaap doesn't see me, then I cross the street running. I have trouble keeping balance on my new heels. As soon as I open the passenger door, the pleasant scent of vanilla hits me in the face. Ah, such a delight. 'Well, well, baby, aren't you looking good?' Hatim compliments me on my new outfit. He seems impressed by my wide zebra leggings, the socks and heels, which are, in fact, one size too small. 'Thank you,' I mumble, bashfully casting down my eyes.

'How was your first day at work?', Hatim wants to know. 'Quite exciting, actually,' I answer, smoothing out my apron with my hands. I decide to leave out the epilation drama with Selma that happened in the salon.

'Babe,' Hatim says and his fingers stroke my cool cheek and my dry lips. What if Jaap sees us like this and tells Boubker everything? Oh well, I'll be marrying Hatim soon anyway, so why would I care? 'Yes, is there something you want to say?' I ask timidly. 'How would you like it if Lala Rosa would be put in your name?' Hatim suddenly says… Lala Rosa? In my name! So, he really does want to marry me! Oh, I can picture it already. Lala Rosa in my name. My property. How much money would I make if I sold the place? Surely it would be enough to pay for my wedding, the Mercedes and the villa. But perhaps, I suddenly think, it's better to keep the place to myself. After all, a single and successful businesswoman has the same status as a married one. And I wouldn't even need that Hatim anymore. I wonder what those village fools would have to say about that? Me, my own company… F'dila, who was first identified as a village witch, returning as a successful businesswoman… But between Hatim and me, there is still Souad's fat ass. That ass will first have to leave the battlefield, as well as his wife Baktha of course. I had completely forgotten about her… If Hatim wants to tie the knot with me, he will first have to divorce Baktha. But the doctor will take care of that.

'Anything you want, Hatim,' I breathe gently into his ear. Would he be serious? His beaming eyes say it all.

'Fasten your seat belt, babe.'

Hatim parks his car on the quay along the water. The view over the Maas river is like a live painting. The quay is quiet and deserted. Except for a man in a faded raincoat and his dog, there isn't a living soul in sight.

It's a tempestuous autumn day and too cold for this time of

year. I close my eyes and listen to the crackle of autumn leaves dancing. It's as if the dry leaves are celebrating. Lala Rosa will soon be mine, I suddenly remember. I can brave anything, the autumn cold, Souad's vicious looks and Boubker's grumbling…

Then, all of a sudden, without a word, Hatim ruthlessly pulls my head forward, I can feel a sharp pain burning in my neck. 'Here, babe!' he orders, breathlessly. Before I understand what he's getting at, he has already opened the button of his jeans. As soon as his zipper goes down, his underwear pops out. The cheesy smell of his genitals penetrates my nose. Lonely raindrops fall down mercilessly. They clatter loudly on the roof of the car and against the car windows. A few seconds later, everything gets steamed up, so we no longer see what is going on outside. For a moment I feel dirty and low, just as my fellow villagers thought I was…

Loud music is booming in the background and I walk into the toilet for the tenth time to rinse my mouth and gargle my throat with water. I fish Hatim's goo out of my apron. I caught it in a tissue. As soon as I got to Lala Rosa, I put the piece of paper in a plastic sandwich bag. I allow myself a short break on the toilet and look at the sandwich bag. I stare at it, as if I'm staring at a goldfish swimming in a sandwich bag filled with water. I can't help noticing that some of the stuff is still wet. The vast majority has already dried up, like dry white snot. I study the leftovers that are still moist and have stuck to the sandwich bag. I once learned that semen lives on for a while. These are in fact mini-Hatims who will be as determined as I am. Could I get pregnant with this stuff? I smell the sandwich bag. The smell of sweet and sour at once reminds me of Mr Professor and how everything had failed miserably.

In the background, the chatter of the ladies is clearly audible, despite the loud music playing and the bellowing of the hair dryers blowing hot air day and night. Then suddenly, without thinking, I run my little finger through the sandwich bag. Deeply fascinated I stare at the living organisms that can result in a real person, yet are invisible to my naked eye. I take a deep breath and…

'Hello!' Suddenly there is a loud banging on the door. I jump up with a start and drop the tissue and sandwich bag on the floor, ssshhooo!

'Yes?' I open the toilet door a little. 'Well, hello,' Souad is standing in front of the door, chewing gum, angrily tapping her hips with her fake nails. 'I've been here for an hour, desperate for a pee and you still haven't finished!' 'I'm sorry,' I tell the bitch, practically vomiting, 'I keep having to throw up and I've just been sick all over the toilet.'

'What? Yuck!' Souad doesn't hide her disgust. 'I'll walk to the bakery next door,' she informs me before decisively pushing the door shut, very nearly crushing my little finger.

Relieved, I rinse my face with cold water at the fountain. The sandwich bag with sperm crackles in my apron.

Nothing is too much to ask.

Even if the sorcerer would have asked me for the hair of a hungry lion, I would have gotten it. This time, nothing is stopping me…

CHAPTER 5

Souad

Twerk like Miley

'Souad, can you open the door? It's like the *hammam* in here!'

With a bang I fling the doors of Lala Rosa wide open. Before long the wedding music floods the crowded shopping street.

Some days we make an exception to the 'women strictly separated from men' rule. Each time the doors of our ladies' hair salon open, the entire neighborhood peeks inside. All those curious passers-by, visiting the market on Thursdays, hordes of women who had always wanted to come in, but never dared to. And those ancient, growly, frustrated men, spitting on the ground to show their bitter aversion to our salon. But it's particularly those Cristiano Ronaldo replicas, the pretty ugly kind, driving by in their Audi, Mercedes or BMW. I wouldn't care if those men wore out the road with their fast cars, because I play those guys like no one else can.

'Look at that nutcase driving by again.' I chew my gum and cut with two scissors, left and right-handed, into the hair of Umma Uggs. In between I swing my hips, while Umma loudly claps her hands, dances with her shoulders and lets out *Zaghrouta* cries. See, my timing is such that I'm completely sure that Audi's driver saw me dancing.

'Sooo, there's that dickhead again,' Layla stops blow-drying to take a good look at the creep in the black BMW.

'There's another one?' Umma asks.

'Don't stare too long at this one, you might end up with post traumatic stress disorder,' I warn Layla.

'Well, where did they dig her up? Some ancient cave?' Umma giggles, nodding at Layla.

'She probably thawed off a melting glacier,' I answer, blowing my bubblegum. 'Well, you know what they say: fortune is a good neighbor moving in,' I sigh. I look at Layla, our future lawyer, who will one day think too much of herself to keep working here. She'll be rolling in money, ugh!

'I think he has driven by about five times now, what's this dickhead's deal?' Layla says, raising her shoulders.

'What do you think?' I answer, 'duh.'

Outside it's crowded with fancy cars. It's getting busier by the minute. 'That other guy in the Audi, he's hot, seriously,' I say as I start swinging my hips again. 'Let me know when you see him, okay?' I order Layla. 'Maybe I can get his number!' I say, and I realize then that this guy must be loaded.

I reach into my tiger skinnies to double-check that all the numbers I scored yesterday haven't accidentally fallen out of my pockets.

'What kind of Audi does he drive, then?' Umma asks me.

'An A-7, *ah*-idiot! An A-7!' I say, as I cheerfully cut into Umma's hair and mine at the same time. Then I check myself in the mirror to see if everything looks alright. 'Ugh, my nail has broken,' I stare at the torn piece of acrylic. 'Isn't that great. I just coughed up 80 euros for these friggin' nails!'

'An A-7? Girl, that guy is loaded!' Umma whisks me out of my angry daydream. She and her worn out Uggs that must be five sizes too big by now. Umma always wears Uggs; summer, winter, fall, it doesn't matter. For all I know the chick will show up at her own wedding wearing those ugly-ass street slippers.

'If you know what I mean,' I say, and I wink at myself in the mirror. In the meantime, I glide my hair back into shape.

'He's about to drive by!' Layla informs me.

'Seriously?'

Then I break into a sweat… A moment later the shiny front of the silver Audi A-7 appears. He moves slowly past the door of the salon, as if everything is happening in slow motion.

I suddenly don't know what to do with myself anymore. But I must get his attention, no matter what. Then, out of the blue, I cast all my self-respect aside, as I do regularly. Without knowing why, I bend my back far forward, so that my hair touches the ground. I spontaneously start twerking! Shaking my behind in the middle of Lala Rosa hair salon for ladies. The customers have no idea what's happening. I'm like Miley Cyrus, except with an ass that's actually impressive. Compared to mine, Miley's is no more than two flatbreads. The woman in the black garment, whom I often refer to as Taliban, starts laughing. '*Ah*-crazy woman!' she says, waving her hands.

'What? Did she fall?' Green Djellaba sips from her coffee.

'No, no, she's dancing… you know, dancing…'

'Dancing? I think she fell forward,' the old lady in the green djellaba waves her hand, dismissing Taliban.

Look, at least my twerk-out is paying off. The Audi, tires squeaking, very nearly scooped an old lady off the crosswalk.

'Well, where was I?' I utter in a sweat, as I feel my backache coming up again. How should I know that twerking is an assault to the spine when I'd never done it before? Oh well, I quickly resume my cutting. I wonder if my twerking had any effect and if Mister Audi will come by to give me his number.

'Is he looking?' I ask Layla from the corner of my eye.
   'You mean is he drooling?'

'I swear,' Umma says to me, 'you really are crazy.'
   I contentedly look at myself in the mirror. 'I am very crazy indeed, but I'll tell you something; what you see is what you get. And I can't exactly say that about most ladies coming here,' I say, and I give Umma a big wink, followed by a chewing gum bubble.
   'You're right about that,' she nods.

'*Ah*-they act like saints, but they are not honest at all.' Taliban bitterly folds her hands. Things are tough for her, the sweetheart.
   'Taliban?' I ask her.
   '*Ah*-my name is not Taliban! You and your Taliban!'
   'I forgot your name again, what is it?'
   'Salsabyl.'
   'My point exactly. How do you expect me to remember a difficult name like that?' I explain to Salsabyl.
   'They're not honest at all,' I repeat her words. Layla remains suspiciously quiet. I don't know why. When it comes to morals, she's usually one of the first to open her mouth. She and her university degree and her emancipation bullshit. To be honest, I think I'm the only emancipated one here. I try to get as much money out of men as possible, but I generally don't need these men themselves for anything.
   'I've been through it myself,' Salsabyl resumes the conversation and bitterly throws her magazine on the table. Salsabyl often has trouble speaking, but at Lala Rosa we agree unanimously; she should talk about her problems if she wants to get over them. 'Yes, yours is a really bad situation,' I say, as I accidentally smack the back of Umma's head with my scissors.

'*Ah*-watch out *ah*-idiot,' Umma covers her head to protect it.

'Oh sorry,' I say to Umma and turn to Salsabyl again, 'I don't know how you manage.' I keep waving my Jaguar scissors.

'What happened?' Umma asks, scratching her head and looking at her hand. 'Seriously, there's a drop of blood here…, *ah*-idiot!'

'Stop overreacting,' I say, and firmly poke her on the shoulder.

'I found my best friend in my own bed with my husband,' Salsabyl suddenly comes straight to the point. She takes her time to recover from the bomb she dropped and adjusts her large black veil. Some women just have that quality, they look great in every hijab and every long robe. Salsabyl looks astonishing in her veil, any kind of couture would pale in comparison. When you are pretty on the inside, you're automatically pretty on the outside, it doesn't matter what you wear. I don't share that kind of stuff with Salsabyl of course, I'd rather keep it to myself.

'You can't be serious,' Umma utters, visibly shaken. Layla stops briefly and turns off her blow-dryer with a pale face. There's a thin layer of sweat on her forehead and she rolls her eyes before taking a big gulp of air. What's going on with this chick?

'But I am,' Salsabyl continues, 'my best friend of all people… I thought of her as my sister and yet she took a little taste of my husband.'

'It's your own fault!' Dijana enters the conversation. Normally, you don't even notice she's there. But whenever she opens her mouth, Dijana is hard and ruthless. Still, even though she's from Eastern Europe, Dijana is always right. She continues

epilating, smoothly rolling a piece of thread across her customer's face, like a lawnmower straightening out unwanted
blades of grass.

'What do you mean, my own fault?'

'I just don't get you women!' Dijana says, swinging the piece
of thread in her hand. 'In my culture, a married woman
doesn't hang out with a unmarried girl. There's the single girl,
frenetically looking for a man. And then there's her girlfriend,
whom she's extremely envious of. 'Cause she does have a
man… of course she's going to steal him! It's always the same
with you women. Each day there's a new one, storming into
the salon crying; "I caught my husband with my girlfriend!" I
am no longer shocked.'

'But it's not what friends do, right?'
    'Look, your best friend is your worst enemy.'
    'They are not honest at all.'
    'How did you catch them again?'
    'Oh, I can't bear thinking about it… Those heels I found in
the hall to begin with, and the noises coming from the bedroom. It was awful!'
    '*Wili, wili*, that's just horrible.'
    'I bet she enchanted him!'
    'I've been through the exact same thing. Everything you've
also been through,' one of the other customers says to Salsabyl.
    'But you are so modern,' Salsabyl looks up, clearly surprised.
    'Being modern is only comparative,' the customer, a politi-
cian, answers.
    'Compra-what? Ah-I don't understand! You always use
such difficult words.'

'Ah-use normal words, we don't understand you!'

'It's always the same with those so-called highly educated people, you don't even know what they're saying!'

'So what did you do?'

'The same he did to me. I took a boyfriend,' the politician says firmly.

'You have all lost your minds, you young people.' Green Djellaba snaps.

'When you do everything for a man, he'll start treating you like trash,' the politician suddenly says fiercely, 'but the moment you properly confront them, all of a sudden they show some respect.'

'You women are always all smiles in the beginning, patronizing your husband, until he starts treating you like a doormat. I fed my husband donkey ears from day one, and I never heard from him once after that,' Green Djellaba says, loudly smacking her hand on the table.

Sometimes it's busy at Lala Rosa, then suddenly it's quiet again. On Friday and Saturday the salon easily transforms into a steamy henhouse. It's teeming with women on those days, from early in the morning until way past closing time. The wait can sometimes add up to five hours. As a hairdresser you're supposed to be on your feet all day, and in my case; you go visit a club afterwards. Gosh, I wonder how I manage.

Layla and Dijana have gone for a stroll at the market. I look at my broken acrylic nail and sigh in boredom. I just don't get why those two idiots are so wild about that market rubbish. I prefer the fancy stuff from Richard Shoes and the whole shebang on the P.C. Hooftstraat in Amsterdam. The kind of clothes and shoes I can't actually afford.

I plop down into my empty chair; I've stuffed countless pieces of my pink gum onto that thing. I take a few big gulps from my Cherry Coke can and let out a shameless, loud burp into the room.

I reach into my tight tiger leggings for my phone which I stuck between my panties and skin.

With sticky fingers I compose a message and send it to Schmeegle, the man I met at the School of Management. He is a lot older than I am, but still; he's so charming and of course highly intelligent. He looks a bit like that actor from Nespresso... one of those older guys I can actually work with... He's got a lot of dough and he's a real gentleman. As we were talking, I noticed what a well-groomed impression he made. And he smelled amazing. His nails were shining and there wasn't a crease in his tailor-made suit.

Schmeegle is one of those classy guys who'll always make you look good. You just know he'll treat you right- and seriously, he has a built-in navigation system in the windshield of his car! A contact like that always comes in handy. You never know what for... And if Schmeegle and I ever get together, I'll just have him converted.

'Hello?' A woman peeks in.

'Yeah?' I answer slightly irritated, because I just don't feel like working.

Instead I sip my coke, swiveling in my hairdresser's chair.

'Are you open?' The woman is middle aged, or she looks much older than she actually is. She's wearing a F'dila-like raincoat and she looks like a F'dila, too, except tall and colossal instead of small and pudgy.

'Duh, of course we're open,' I answer casually. She's hovering at the doorstep.

'Do you always leave the door open?' she asks, hesitantly stepping into the salon.

'No, but we were melting, you know,' I say. Everyone knows the Lala Rosa doors are often open on Thursdays, everyone knows that, right?

I lead the F'dila-like woman to the waiting table. 'Just take a seat until I'm ready.' The table is deserted and there's no one else waiting. Still, I take my time to drink the Cherry Coke, it's not like we get any breaks here.

The woman looks awkward as she takes a seat at the waiting table. It's weird, I've never seen her here before. Not even on the street, I would have recognized her instantly. The standard here is; everybody knows everybody, even if you know nobody or are a nobody.

'Where are you from?' I ask the woman.

'From Oudja,' she answers, 'you?'

'I mean here, where are you from around here?'

'Oh, from the Northern part of Rotterdam,' she says as she takes her hijab off.

Oh my, it's obvious she has never visited a hairdresser before. Never in her life.

'That explains why I've never seen you around here before.'

'Exactly, I've never been here before... Are those jewels in the showcase real?', the woman asks.

'Nothing is real,' I explain. And that's exactly how it is; everything you see here is fake, false and forged. It's the look that matters.

'So, what do you want me to do with your hair?' I ask her.

'My hair?'

'Or are you here for an epilation?'

'I actually don't know,' the woman scratches her head.

Her curly hair lays flat on her head. It's frizzy and looks like old Angora wool.

'Well, at least let me do your split ends, because this really won't do anymore.' I take a final sip of my coke. I put the can down on the coffee table and walk towards the woman to take a better look.

I would almost swear she's frightened. The way she clutches the cheap handbag on her lap, as if I'd want to rob her. 'Will you let me look at your face for a minute?' I ask her. I take her face into my hand, the prickles in her chin are piercing my fingers.

'Do you think I need an epilation?' the woman asks.

'No doubt about it,' I say directly.

'Just my upper lip?' the woman squeaks. Then I turn her face from left to right for better lighting. 'Your entire face, you look like an angora rug on feet,' I say as I let her face slip out of my hands.

'Will it hurt?' the woman asks. She caresses her cheeks, searching for the little hairs she obviously never noticed before.

'Is this your first epilation with string?'

'Yes,' she answers timidly.

'*Ah*-you're going to be scared shitless!'

It looks like she's trying to swallow a dry piece of straw.

'What's your name, anyway?' I ask.

'It's Baktha.'

'Come here, Baktha.' I pull the pointed comb out of my tiger skinnies and start combing Baktha's hair. I soon realize she regularly treats her hair with henna. Despite all those split ends her hair still feels healthy and it shines beautifully.

'Do you have kids?' I decide to interrogate her. You see, I have this hunch... Then I get my Jaguar scissors out of my pants and start cutting the split ends.

'Yes, three... what about you?' Baktha then asks me.

'Of course not, I don't even have a man... do you?' I suddenly stop cutting.

'I'm married.'

'Oh, thank goodness, most women who come here are divorced… do you have a happy marriage?' I ask, and fetch a pack of Bubblicious from the table in front of me.

'Oh well, as soon as you're married your husband gives you the cold shoulder, especially when kids come into the picture,' she dismisses my question.

'Oh, that sucks,' I say, and put a fresh piece of gum into my mouth. See, it's always same old, same old around here.

'These days it's better to be the woman on the side, they're the ones men actually treat well,' I give the woman a wink. To put her at ease I say; 'you are a beautiful woman, I don't know why that idiot doesn't pay attention to you. Maybe it'll help if you go for a shorter cut and some highlights.' I take a good look at her in the mirror. She's not an unattractive woman at all, on the contrary; she's a beautiful woman, she just needs a bit more maintenance.

'So, if you were to give me a tip to change my look, what would that be?'

'Well, for starters, the raincoat,' I say, casually pointing my scissors at the coat rack. 'You look like a F'dila,' I say, adding a little extra, 'just add an apron and a pair of supermarket scissors and you'd be her exact look-alike.'

'Who is F'dila?' Baktha asks, indignantly.

'Hatim's cousin… oh, never mind.'

'You mean Hatim, the owner,' she turns to face me.

'Ah, you know him?' I ask her, as I turn the hairdresser's chair back into place and use my pointed comb to part her hair. 'Hatim is the manager, so to say. The business is in the name of his wife, but we never see her around here. In fact: no one has ever even seen her at all.'

'What? In the name of his wife?' the woman yells, throwing her hands into her lap as she turns to face me again.

'Come on, hold still already, I've just created a nice parting,' I say, turning her to face the mirror again.

'Oh, sorry,' she answers.

'It's just the business isn't in his wife's name at all,' Baktha says, shaking her head.

'Can't you sit still?' I poke her shoulder. 'Hang on, did you say not in his wife's name? What do you mean?'

'Well, exactly what I said. I'm his wife. There is no way this business is in my name.'

'But in whose name is it then?' I manage, my gum almost slipping out of my mouth.

'Maybe you can tell me,' Baktha suddenly pulls a surly face.

'Wow, wow!' I exclaim, throwing my arms backwards, 'the business really isn't in *my* name, chill!' I clench my teeth and draw another parting into Baktha's hair. But whose name *is* it in? Is this really Hatim's wife?

In the small toilet of Lala Rosa I use a wet towel to rub the mascara off my fake lashes. Then I put the long skirt over my tiger leggings, fetch the large tiger print hijab out of my bag and drape it over my head like a saint. It's not that everybody thinks I normally wear a hijab, but I'm visiting my aunt and I would rather not listen to her whining. You know, she's the kind of aunt who's like 'all women are evil...' I've actually never heard her speak positively about other women. In that way she's not unlike the women coming here.

Well then, looking decent again.

'Bye bye!' I greet everyone and storm out of the salon, before anyone gets a chance to comment on my transformation from tiger miniskirt to tiger leggings, to tiger print hijab.

I'm about to cross the road and the tram tracks to the other side of the street where my old Ford Fiesta is parked, when I feel a few raindrops softly falling on my face. The car is still exactly where I left it yesterday morning. I look for my car keys in my purse and find them between a stack of banknotes. I consider giving the money to my mother, like I always do. Then I get distracted by a man waiting by my dark blue Fiesta.

'What are you doing here?' I ask, as larger raindrops fall onto my make-up free face.

'*Wili, wili,* what are you wearing?' Hatim notices, pointing at my hijab.

'Move over,' with my hips I mercilessly push him aside, so I can reach my car door. I casually sit down behind the wheel and slam the door of my little car shut.

Hatim stubbornly keeps tapping the window. 'Baby, what's with you?' he asks as I open up the window. 'What's with me is I'm in a hurry.' I'm always like this with Hatim. Somehow men do start showing more respect when you treat them this curtly.

'How would you feel if Lala Rosa was put in your name?' Hatim asks me beaming, challenging, tantalizing… He looks at me in all possible ways.

'What?' my eyes almost pop out of their sockets.

'That means you would be the owner, babe,' he throws me his most charming smile and a wink.

'Get in,' I command, 'but I don't have a lot of time. I have to visit my aunt in a minute.'

CHAPTER 6

Layla

On My Own

'Layla, dinner!' my youngest brother yells from the staircase.

'Not hungry! Homework!' I fume back from my bedroom. I am in my pink pajamas, computer on my lap, trying to write my thesis.

'Are you coming?' my youngest sister knocks on the door.

'I am doing my homework, *ah*-idiot!' I snap.

'Come eat, my girl!' my mother, too, yells from downstairs.

'Homework, not hungry!'

Really, it's impossible to get anything done here, with all these chatterboxes constantly interrupting. I mean, seriously, how am I supposed to focus on my work? How am I going to write my damn thesis? It's like day care here with all these siblings around. Oof, and those wiggly letters on the screen and my notebook's bright light shining into my eyes… What am I supposed to do? And why on earth am I listening to *Losing my Religion*? That's a recipe for depression… 'Oooh,' I sigh, rubbing my head… I have to deliver my thesis in a month, no matter what.

I can't get myself more awake than this. The coffee remedy didn't do a thing and my job at Lala Rosa is really starting to take its toll. Since the lectures have finished, I work there every day, and at home I sit behind my laptop until the early hours. Honestly, it's no longer doable, and soon it will be even worse. Once I have my degree, working at Lala Rosa will be impossible to combine with the three-year internship I must do before I'm allowed to start my own law firm. Ahh, that would be amazing. My own office and my own apartment. I'm certain my parents, family, acquaintances and friends won't mind me living on my own once I've earned my status as a lawyer. Because hard cash smashes every taboo. Oh, what a treat it would be, all the quiet and freedom in my own home. With my own interior, my own taste. I was thinking pastel shades with colorful accessories and big vases filled with orchids. Aah, to decide for myself what's for dinner, to plan my own holidays. And I'll have a Mini Cooper convertible… What a relief to look forward to.

I put on the song *On My Own*. Typing suddenly goes very smoothly and I sing along at the top of my lungs.

You don't think I got fire
I'll tell you: I will survive

'Hey! This isn't Club Cinema, *ah*-idiot!' my younger sister bangs on the door loudly, 'What do you think, that you're at Lala Rosa? Turn it down! Don't you have any respect? Your father is praying in the other room, *ah*-idiot!'

'Oh, shut up' I yell at the door, but decide to put on my headphones. It *is* disrespectful to blast music and sing along loudly, while my father is praying in the other room… I realize I still have to do my prayers.

I'm starting to get into party mode. I picture myself clubbing as I type with one hand and swipe the other through the air like I'm standing in Club VIP with a can of soda. Then I type quickly, only to stop again after a moment to wildly shake my head, shoulders, and my butt. Yesss, now we're getting somewhere, I'm going to write my thesis and get my degree, I'm gonna make it....

I'm gonna do this
On my own now!

A smile appears on my face, followed by a loud sob. I grab a Kleenex from the box on the bed. I empty my nose into it and catch my tears. What if Hatim goes on like this?

I close my laptop.

Each day a new tax notice arrives, and to make matters worse, there's an overflow of envelopes from debt collection agencies, too! My parents *cannot* find out about this, whatever happens. But how much longer will I be able to hide all this? What if they come to clear out our house? I'll never be able to show my face here again, I'll fossilize slowly into a dried-out pile of clay.

So far, I've managed to convince my parents that all those assessments are for my studies and they've gotten used to them. Tax forms have been coming in on a weekly basis. 'I really don't understand why the government is so tough on students. They're really starting to lose it now,' my dad said the other day. The sweetheart. If only he knew.

Since I told Hatim I want out of this deal, he has deliberately stopped paying the bills. 'No way,' he told me over the phone, coldly, 'you're staying.' He is intentionally getting me into trouble, just to bully me. As if he's getting a kick out of it.

Hatim, you asshole, you have plenty of money and still you

act like this! I hate you! Accidentally, I knock over my laptop, which rolls over the bed and falls on the carpet.

I have to see Hatim. I don't want Lala Rosa in my name anymore, I can't afford it any longer…

I must get myself out of this situation quickly. Although, perhaps there's something else I can use Hatim for? He has a lot of money, and if he doesn't want me to get out of Lala Rosa then maybe I can get him to invest in my future law firm?

Lost in thought, I put my laptop beside me on the purple duvet cover and rub my chin until it turns red. It will take another three years before I'm allowed to open my office, but I could get the money now. Then I'll put it aside for later.

It's high time for a new strategic phase… with Hatim as my main sponsor.

'Layla, are you coming for dinner?' my dad asks, softly tapping his fingers on my door. 'Do you want to stay in your room? You *have* to eat something, my girl.'

'I'm coming,' I tell my father.

Hatim doesn't usually respond when I text him but we have to speak urgently. And this message should do the trick…

I need you
so badly.
xLaylaLove

Hatim never really accepted the fact that I ended our relationship when I found out he was married. Nonetheless, he kept paying for my studies and I agreed to put Lala Rosa in my name as sole proprietor. That's how greedy I was back then, and that's how greedy I actually still am. After finishing hairdresser college I worked in the salon at daytime, and studied part time in the evenings. Later, I combined my full-time master's program with working at Lala Rosa, too.

Before long I get a response from Hatim:

Where? When?
xHatim

I am determined to make hay while the sun shines.

Breakaway 8pm this evening?
Like we used to.
xLaylaLove

Upon which Hatim responds:

See you tonight babe
xHatimLikeWeUsedTo

My mother's tajine tastes excellent… but I have to hurry now, so I quickly brush my teeth in the bathroom and squeeze myself into the black jeans I just ironed. On top of that I wear a big studded belt, a grey T-shirt with a faded picture of Brigitte Bardot and black sleek sneakers. I let my hair fall out of its bun and ruffle it back into shape. I leave out the make-up for now, just like I used to.

Golden red autumn leaves are drifting everywhere; they color the evening and land in sticky piles along the road. Suddenly big cold raindrops are falling on my face, so the water literally streams across my cheeks. Cycling in these harsh weather conditions is impossible.

As I arrive at Breakaway, soaking wet down to my underwear, I try to find a free table. But the table will take a while, so I stand and wait at the bar. In the meantime I wipe the rain out of my hair with a tissue and order a portion of nachos with jalapenos and melted cheese. The cold and cycling always make me hungry. Oh well, Hatim is paying anyway, so, 'you know what, make it two.'

I'm surrounded by loud music, hordes of foreign students and the walls are decorated with Harley Davidson bikes. After waiting for a few minutes, I am shown an empty table. The handsome waiter takes my order, 'one pineapple juice,' and the nachos are placed in front of me.

I hesitate if I should leave some for Hatim, like I used to… but I can't control my hunger. 'What the heck.' One after another, I cram the delicious guacamole-covered nachos into my mouth. 'One more!' I point at the plate. Oh well, Hatim is paying.

Hatim and I used to come here all the time. We would sit upstairs at the pool tables, or on the balcony, with a romantic view over the walkway. We always had a great time; I was in the flow and Hatim, for his part, was crazy in love with me. We had all kinds of wild plans, like a holiday to Ibiza and buying an apartment with a nice view over the Maas river and the skyline of Rotterdam. How should I have known he was already married? With two children, or was it three? Well, it doesn't matter anymore anyway.

If it were up to Hatim, we would still be together. Then I would have lived on the riverside, in my yuppie apartment. At least, if he would have been able to convince my parents. How was he even planning on asking them for my hand, without mentioning he was already married? What was he thinking?

I munch away the last nachos, all soft by now, drenched in tomato juice and avocado sauce. Hatim really should have been here by now. Restlessly, I look at my bright pink watch. Then I raise my finger. 'Another pineapple juice, please.' A little later I start drinking my third glass of juice as if my life depends on it. I down it in one go. 'Ugh!'

'Don't like your juice?' the waiter asks me, clearly surprised.

'No, no, it's good,' I assure him.

Hatim, where are you?

Two hours later. I'm about to explode. I should never have eaten so many nachos, especially after the tajine I already had at home. Hatim didn't show, I'll have to deal with the bill and I still don't have a solution for Lala Rosa. And the worst part is I didn't get to work on my thesis. Oh, I feel miserable... So stupid! I struggle not to burst into tears on the spot.

Something has to happen, you see. Without asking, the waiter puts another glass of pineapple juice on the table. 'Thanks,' I say kindly.

There must be a way to win Hatim over. It's high time for serious measures. Perhaps even for visiting a medicine man, a sorcerer. You know... Just to help change my luck a little... I realize I don't have any other choice.

CHAPTER 7

F'dila

My victims

'F'dila, you're a genius,' I tell myself out loud. My fingers contentedly glide across the plastic sandwich bag with the crumpled tissue. Smug as a dehydrated stray cat who just found water, I am sitting on the hard stool in the waiting room. Smug, yet a little impatient. I did exactly what the sorcerer told me to do. I am very curious how strong the spell will be. And in what form will he give me the voodoo? Will I have to stir something in someone's dinner? Or dip the hand of a corpse in a plate of food before my victims eat from it? Will I have to bury something in a child's grave again?

Oh, what will it be this time? A fire letter or an amulet I must carry with me? Or does this man do all the hocus-pocus remotely? You see, you never really know with a healer. Whether or not everything will work out with a spell has to do with various factors beyond your own control. Like magic.... how strong, for instance, is that? How powerful is his sorcery? Has he been to a sorcerers' school or is he a schizophrenic who has suddenly connected with spirits and started fortune-telling? Or is it perhaps hereditary?

Another determining factor for the success of a spell has to do with the victim himself. If Hatim is wearing an anti-voodoo amulet, it will be a difficult task. It is also important that

I perform the ritual on Hatim at a moment when no one else does voodoo on him. Two or more magic components can cancel one another. Suppose I do voodoo on Hatim and at the same time his wife Baktha does it, or, worse even, Souad, then Hatim might completely lose his mind. I fear this is what happened to Boubker. The poor sod who just climbed on a rooftop one day and scattered his fortune over the city. He probably deflowered some chick and then didn't marry her. This is often the case with virgins who fell for it. Men promise a wedding, the women are deflowered and then dropped like a ton of bricks. The revenge of a dumped virgin is often crude. To be sure my spells work on Hatim, I will visit the healer as often as I can. The more dark rituals performed, the better. I really hope the voodoo will do something and my dreams will come true. It's like the lottery; one day fortune might just fall into your lap.

If the voodoo does not work out well, there is always plan C. I wonder if the little bit of Hatim's semen that I inserted in myself has had any effect… Could I be pregnant? How would Hatim react to the news? Would he reject me? I'll just force him to take a DNA test! If it has been determined that I have a child of his, he can no longer reject me! Many women have hooked a man this way. If they can do it, so can I.

The waiting room is narrow, musty and oppressively warm. The long queue runs from the top to the bottom of the stairs and it's teeming with women here. They all come here for a wonder drug. We are the Cinderellas of our own imagination and the sorcerer is the fairy godfather fulfilling all our wishes. Most of them simply come here to tie their men to them, like mountain mules with pack saddles and muzzles. Married or unmarried, that doesn't matter nowadays. Or they come to take revenge on their horrible ex, a girlfriend, neighbor, niece, aunt or any random stranger they dislike. Voodoo fixes everything for them, even though they're not allowed to use it.

Below my feet, the thick carpet itches uncomfortably. Phew, I hate waiting… And I worry someone will see and recognize me here. Before you know it, they'll call me 'village witch' again.

To hide myself as much as possible, I pull my hijab over my head like an improvised *burqa* and gaze at the large birch outside the window where sparrows are singing to the morning. You can only see my back and my face is no longer recognizable.

'Pheeeeew!', I manage, gasping for air, I've never been good at small dusty spaces. I decide to escape this narrow, stuffed waiting room and make my way to the drafty corridor. The wait will not be much longer, because I can be called any moment now for my consultation with the doctor.

Once in the hall, I stare at the carpet as innocently as possible. With the same look I always put on when I walk the street with Boubker. This way I create the impression that I am innocent. 'Oh, oh!' I say and press my hands in my back, 'I'm in such pain… Flames, I feel flames rising all day long.' 'You too, girl?' says an old woman, shaking her head. The other ladies nod as well, then stare at the ground again. 'That's my daughter over there, she was fed voodoo, look at her now!'

To be on the safe side, I don't look at her daughter. She might be possessed by a ghost and before you know it the ghost might leap over to me if I were to look her in the eye. Then I can forget about my wedding, my Mercedes and my impressive villa. 'That's why I always say; never dine with strangers,' and I squeeze the woman's upper arm very hard to warn her.

'You know what you should do?' I counsel the woman. 'Grab

a cup, pee in it and let your daughter drink it all up. Then all the voodoo will go away on its own.' I clap my hands together and give the woman a firm wink. By nature, I am a peaceful person who likes helping others. If I hadn't been so busy with my job as a hairdresser at Lala Rosa, I might have opened my own practice and become a medicine woman. It's a booming business, you see, where a lot of money can be made.

'Gosh, you're good,' the woman says. 'You must have a lot of experience…' 'Oh, you have no idea what I've been through,' I tell the woman. 'I was a housekeeper for two professors in the city back home. They treated me like a slave. One day, Mr Professor tried to grope me and his wife took her revenge by feeding me a voodoo powder,' I make it up on the spot. With my wide skirt and my embroidered apron, I must sound very convincing. 'Poor thing,' the woman says and she sympathetically rubs my back with her hand. It feels soft and pleasant.

Moments later, a ghastly silence dominates the hallway, occasionally interrupted by a strange kind of whinny. 'That lady in the waiting room is possessed by a horse spirit,' the old woman explains. 'Is that so?' I instantly wonder if I could let Souad be possessed by the ghost of a camel or a cow. I can already picture her ruminating on her chewing gum… I'm sure Hatim will no longer pay her any attention. He will only have to focus on me and I will only have to focus on Lala Rosa, which will very soon be my property. But what to do with his wife Baktha?

'Phew,' I sigh deeply. Although I arrived here at 5:15 am sharp, I've been waiting for over three hours by now. A few people were already waiting on the street when I arrived. As soon as the door opened, everyone started to push and squeeze. It's like Lala Rosa, where the wait can easily take hours.

I really want to knock at the door, but I'm too afraid… He might get cross with me and I still need him. This healer is very skillful when it comes to sorcery, the women here tell me. He can turn water into ice, so he must be absolutely amazing. A rock star.

Soon after, the silence in the hallway is drowned out by squeaking hinges and a lot of creaking. The door seems to open by itself. I quickly put my hands in my apron, so at least I look virtuous and submissive. I am a virtuous and submissive woman after all… This sorcerer must not think I'm some sort of village witch…

And suddenly he's there, the ancient man, blind as a bat, aviator sunglasses on the rim of his nose. His beard is knotty and his faded djellaba is woven from a nondescript color of wool. 'So, who is next?', he calls out, upon which the old man forcefully beats his bamboo stick against the wall. Hopefully he won't use it to hit me? Some doctors do, they just beat you to a pulp with their stick; to expel the ghosts, the voodoo or the evil eye from your body. I bring out a bottle of water and, shaken, take a sip. Well, if it needs to happen, it needs to happen. I'll really do whatever it takes to celebrate my wedding extravaganza in our village and to get to my Mercedes and villa. And first I need Hatim and Lala Rosa for that. With or without the beating.

Hesitantly, I walk through the crowd of women in the hallway, following the ancient blind man. I wonder what this trick will cost me.

We sit on the ground on a few sheepskins, facing each other. The office is dark and lit by candle stubs. The scents of burnt lemon stone and more smells dominate the room. My hands are all sweaty, that's how excited I am. The blind healer is throwing cowrie shells out of a leather cup and onto the floor, then picks them up again. He repeats these actions several times. 'I see you have already come very far.'

'Yes, mister.' Gosh, this man is goood!

'You are having a hard time now,' the doctor sighs, then chucks the shells back on the ground. Now the fortuneteller starts shaking his head forcefully.

'Will I ever get my wedding, my house and my car in our village?' I ask him desperately. I will give anything for revenge on those calling me 'village witch'. One by one they will succumb, consumed by jealousy!

'All your dreams will come true; I'll personally see to that. But first we have to make sure that you are no longer bothered by your colleagues, who are also trying to get their hands on Lala Rosa!'

'Souad,' I say sharply.

'Yes, Souad. Don't worry about that,' he reassures me.

The grudge in my abdomen is so agonizing that the pain is rushing to my back. Ooh, I could hurt that bitch so badly!

The sorcerer is now dragging the large earthenware incense burner towards him. It is full of smoldering charcoal and the burnt remains of incense stones. 'Take off your underpants and come stand above this burner quickly!' the man orders me sternly. 'Lift your skirt up high and spread your legs as wide as possible, so the smoke can really come to you,' he continues.

Somewhat embarrassed, I strip myself of my leggings and my underpants, which I haven't had the chance to change this morning. I try to swallow my shame; I have no other choice but to lift my skirt. The guy is blind anyway.

I sigh deeply and take my place above the burning pile of charcoal. The smoke is suffocating and overwhelming, but also smells quite nice.

Here I am. My veil is over my head and my naked snatch right in the face of the healer. First the man has to laugh, the old goat, but soon vague words flow out of his mouth and more incense stones go into the burner and up in smoke. The man speaks words I cannot understand, but I am sure they will have a magical effect and the voodoo will help me get all the things I want. Most importantly, revenge on my fellow villagers.

The suffocating smoke hits my bare delicates and thighs like blazing steam and penetrates my nose and mouth. Boubker should have seen me like this.

'Ugh! Ugh!'

'Come and sit down again,' the doctor orders me. I clear my throat several times and pick my cream-colored underpants up from the floor. I pull my leggings back up.

As soon as I've sat my smoked snatch down on the sheep-skin, he asks me, 'Did you bring that thing I asked for when we spoke on the phone?'

'Yes sir, mister sorcerer,' I say, reaching into my shoulder bag.

The crumpled man holds out his arm and I drop the little sandwich bag with the paper tissue into his hand.

First, he begins to laugh loudly, 'With this…' the doctor says, and then he coughs a few times on Hatim's wrapped stuff. 'With this I make sure that your beloved leaves his wife and marries you. I will also give you a fire letter for Hatim and his wife, so that the one can no longer stand the other. We have to do this thoroughly.' I listen carefully to the words of the doc-tor, who is now working with his cowrie shells again. 'Well,' says the man, 'problems at work, I see.' He asks the question before I can: 'Perhaps we can do something about that too?'

'Yes, that would be great!' I shout. Would he have a spell that makes you better at cutting and epilating?

The healer grins and, as if he can read my mind, says: 'I see that the hair salon will very soon be yours. Isn't that nice?'

'What? Have you really seen that…? I will become the owner of Lala Rosa! Isn't that wonderful!' And if anyone deserves it, it's me! I knew it!

'I will make sure that all goes smoothly, because there's a lot of competition at the moment. I will make sure the entire business is put in your name and all income will become yours. I will give you something, something very strong, so you can also get rid of that Souad… But, there's a price for that,' the he says sternly and starts rattling the shells in his cup again.

'Name it, I'll pay anything,' I quickly say, folding my arms firmly across my chest. I'll sell my body in the local club, if I have to… I'll do anything to realize my ideals and fulfill my dreams.

'Five thousand euros.'

'What! That much?'

'Listen, dear girl. Do you or don't you want a wedding, Mercedes and a villa? Do you or don't you want to take revenge on your fellow villagers? Do you want Hatim, or do you not? Do you want Lala Rosa in your name or not? And Souad, you want her out of the way or not? You tell me.'

'Does it really have to be that expensive?' I say, uneasily putting my fists in the pockets of my apron. I don't know if I can even get that much money.

'You know that this work asks a lot from me. For a job as big as this one, I have to unleash spirits – they will be doing the work for me. And something like that demands extreme precision, which requires a lot of my energy. These things simply cost a lot of money and besides, I always give a guarantee on the spells I make for my customers,' the sorcerer says and he puts the cowrie shells in his cup one by one.

'Guarantee?' I ask skeptically.

The man doesn't answer, instead he goes on to say, 'And what about all those exotic ingredients, I ship in from all over the world. Did you think that was easy? But, F'dila, as I said, the choice is yours.'

I'm not sure. Then suddenly the room fills up with the smell of sweet tea. What a lovely scent... My doubt slips away with the aroma. 'Alright, but on one condition; I want everything as I say it. To start with, I want Souad handled thoroughly,' I tell the man. 'I want her to become possessed by a camel or a cow spirit. Can you arrange that for me?'

'We can arrange that,' the old man mumbles, pressing his aviator sunglasses back into place.

'I want one of those voodoo dolls for Souad, like you see in the movies. So I can stick needles in it when I want to. Can you do that too?'

'If you want one of those dolls, you will get one of those dolls,' and the doctor starts rattling the cup again. 'But I will need a few things for that,' he says sternly. 'Such as?' I ask him doubtfully. 'First of all, something personal from her, like a wisp of hair...,' the man has not even finished speaking before I interrupt him.

'You want hair, here is Souad's hair,' I say and I search my bag for the sandwich bag with Souad's hair in it.

'Where did you get that?' he asks, surprised.

'Yesterday she happened to be cutting her split ends and I picked them up. You want Souad's hair, here it is. Should you want a whisker of a wild tiger or lion, I can arrange that for you too.'

'You little devil.'

When I set my heart on something, I am always well pre-pared. 'But,' I ask the healer skeptically. 'Are you sure you can arrange Souad's voodoo doll?'

'What do you think, that I'm performing some amateur magic show here? My sorcery is no laughing matter!' he says, suddenly annoyed.

I don't want to insult the man any further, or else he will take revenge on me. 'Great,' I say, as a matter of civility. 'I cannot wait for the voodoo doll.'

'Yes, your voodoo doll.' The old man thoughtfully strokes his beard.

'And Hatim,' I continue, 'I want him such that when I say 'go left' his head turns left and when I say 'right', it turns right. I want to own the salon on very short notice. The same goes for my wedding, my Mercedes and the whole shebang. I want everything sooner rather than later. And I want a guarantee… So, mister healer, what will it be?'

He picks his cowrie shells up from the floor and starts to rattle the cup, the way a toddler plays with his toy. Then all kinds of puzzling spells pour out of his mouth. The doctor speaks louder, faster and fiercer… I seem to get into a kind of trance. Out of nowhere I feel a cool gust of wind pass over my back, the hairs on my body are standing on end. Suddenly the candles go out… Petrified, I see the strings of smoke from the extinguished candles rocking and dancing! My heart is in my mouth.

—

CHAPTER 8

Souad

The orphan mouse

'How do you like this one?' I ask from the fitting room in my favorite bling bling-store. Richard Shoes really has it all: cool sneakers, awesome platform heels, tiger tops and skinny jeans in all shapes and sizes. But Hatim isn't looking. Instead, he's staring at his iPhone, absent-mindedly scrolling. It is raining WhatsApp messages – so annoying. Who's that nutcase texting anyway?! I fling the curtain open to get his attention, show off my naked legs and walk around the store like a Victoria's Secret model – except with lots of ass and actual hips. When it comes to quality proportions, those Secret-models have nothing on me.

The dress I'm wearing is tight and made of real leather. It's really a Souad kind of dress. Nonetheless, it has a fancy fit and a real Chanel-vibe. In front of the mirror, I wave my golden blonde, Beyonce-like hair back into shape. Then I pout my lips and pull some sexy posing tricks. I look so cool; you would think I'm in a photo shoot! Hatim's face turns red and his eyes are wide open.

'Well, what do you think?' I ask, daringly.

I was barely able to close the zipper on this dress. It's like I could burst out of it at any moment, and perhaps I will. I wouldn't be surprised…

Hatim remains speechless.

'Alright, then,' I say, 'will you at least help me open the zipper?' I ask, then turn my back toward the crackerhead. Without hesitation Hatim moves closer and with a careful hand opens the stiff zipper on the dress. The nutcase who is about to make all my dreams come true keeps staring at my bare back for a moment or two. I realize once again how easy it is to manipulate men. Seriously, if only I would've found the right one, I would have been married a long time ago.

'And?' the shop assistant asks, poking her head around the corner.

'Hey, could you help take this thing off?' I say and beckon the woman towards the red fitting room. Moments later the shop assistant and I are in a kind of tussle in the narrow booth – you can almost hear Hatim blush.

'I can't breathe! Can't you pull a little harder?' I scream.

'Careful! You'll tear the dress!' the shop assistant orders, frantically attempting to temper my tantrum.

'Oh, I'm all out of breath!' Phew! Seconds later I'm finally out of the dress.

'Do you want me to look for a bigger size?' the shop assistant asks. She carefully folds the cocktail dress over her arm, her fingers caressing the soft leather.

'No, thanks,' I say, annoyed, and wiggle myself into my tight tiger print T-shirt. 'The dress is fine, I'll take it.'

'How are you planning to go about it then?' I ask, my thoughts only half with Hatim and his Kim Jong-un haircut. The other half is admiring the new collection of sleek sneakers. They are covered with lots of bling, which I absolutely love.

'First I have to…' but I interrupt him before he gets a chance to finish answering my question.

'Would you look at those heels! Those are really wicked! No, seriously, they're totally cool! What are those?' I ask the shop assistant.

'They're those platform heels from, what's that singer's name again?'

'Lady Gaga,' I say, blissfully happy, and give the woman a wink.

'Look, how cool is that?' I tell Hatim, 'A heel without a heel! Shall I try them on?'

With a big smile the shop assistant hands me the velvet platform heels without heels. My jaw drops and my eyes transform into those of a greedy magpie. Hatim disappears into the background, as if he was never really there.

'My god, they're gorgeous.'

'How are you planning to go about it then?' I ask Hatim again. We've been waiting at the cash desk for a while next to the pile of cocktail dresses, the high sleek sneakers and Lady Gaga's platform heels without heels. While the shop assistant scans all the items, I stare at the floor and dawdle with my bag, looking for my wallet. This way, the bill will automatically get paid. Hatim will probably pay everything, the idiot.

'Tell me,' I ask him, pushy this time.

'Wait one sec,' Hatim tells me with a firm hand gesture. The shop assistant hands him five bags- along with the long receipt.

Once we're outside with a strong wind coming towards us, Hatim is finally able to give an explanation.

'First, my wife has to put the business in your name, that's all.'

'Your wife?' I exclaim, and instantly stop walking. 'Hatim, can you come clean already? I wasn't born yesterday, okay?!' I say, picking a fight. Exactly who does this nutcase think I am? Some kind of clown?

'What's the matter with you, keep walking.' Hatim pulls the sleeve of my cardigan.

'Hey, don't you touch me!' I tell him in the middle of the street, where all the passers-by can enjoy the show. I don't give a shit about anything or anyone.

'Baby, what's wrong?'

'You know damn well what I'm talking about.'

'Babe, I really don't know what you mean. Come on, keep walking.'

'I'm talking about your wife and the business, which is anything *but* in her name. So why are you trying to trick me?'

Shopping bag in hand, Hatim agitatedly rubs his hair. 'What do you want me to say?'

'Well, for starters I'd like to know whose name Lala Rosa is in. I want you to be honest with me!'

We get ready to walk on towards Hatim's BMW, parked directly across from The Great Chickadee, the grilled chicken restaurant.

'Is it someone in the salon? Is it one of the hairdressers?' I ask him, pushy, but he refuses to answer. His eyes, however, speak volumes.

'You know what,' I tell Hatim, 'I don't wanna know… Babe.' Then I give the man who's gonna make my dreams come true a big fat wink. With a lot of effort Hatim sticks his hand into my skinny jeans, in the middle of the crowded street. All the bags he's carrying luckily cover up my butt.

'Oh!' It makes me giggle. 'Get it together!' I exclaim, and slap that nutcase off me, 'what if someone sees us?'

'Just you wait, you devilish girl, just wait until we're alone.'

'Finally,' I sigh. Calmly, with the fancy bags from Richard Shoes in my hand, I swing the doors of Lala Rosa open. 'Buh-bye,' I wave sweetly to that crackerhead with the Kim Jong-un haircut. At the same moment Hatim speeds away in his BMW... The nutcase isn't ugly, not at all... Hatim's actually quite handsome and attractive. It's just that there's something eerie about him, you know? Something I can't quite put my finger on.

I struggle to keep my balance on the stairs, then slip drastically, but don't fall. It's like I accidentally stepped on a withered banana peel. Phew, lucky that went well.

'Jeez, what is that?' I make a face. Dirty crap, really, under my shoe? Oh, no! Hell no! Ugh, I *just* got these Prada heels... I hate dogshit! I hate it! And I also think I sprained my ankle a little. I'm afraid to look, but I have to... I catch a glimpse of the sole of my shoe and notice there's some white sludge on it. Butter? The tracks I leave on the tiles are covered with the white stuff too. Or is it pigeon poop? I blow a bubble with my gum, wipe my soles on the tiles, and walk my sore ankle to the kitchen. There I see myself to a strong cup of Senseo coffee.

'Dear people, what is this?!' Dijana bawls from the doorstep. She is staring at the floor in dismay, heaps of Primark bags with all her stuff in her hands.

'I almost broke my ankle just then! You have to be careful, it's really slippery,' I tell Dijana, 'you want some coffee?'

'Love some... but I'm not cleaning that.'

'Me neither, just let that F'dila clean it,' I tell Dijana who has begun to prepare her epilation station.

Once I'm in charge here, everything will be different. I can't wait to finally own this place... Whose name is Lala Rosa in, anyway? Dijana seems unlikely. There's no connection whatsoever between her and Hatim. The two don't even talk to each other. F'dila? I don't know. It's very probable, I'm almost certain in fact, that F'dila is here illegally. No doubt about it, so that means the business can't be in her name. Would it be Layla… that hypocrite bitch!

'Souad, come quickly!'

'Now what?!' I sigh from the narrow kitchen. It has been nothing but headache upon headache around here lately. Oh, I could really use a night of fun at the club.

'Here, there, look!' Dijana points at my working station. Seriously, there's henna scattered everywhere; on the floor, the hairdresser's chair, even on the mirror table! And only around *my* working station. My heart is racing… What *is* this?!

Panicking, I run to the kitchen and pull my cell phone out of my skinnies. It rings a few times, but there's no answer. Just as I'm about to give up, he finally picks up the phone.

'Who is this?' the medicine man asks, curtly.

'Hello, it's Souad.'

'Souad who?'

'Wili, Beardman. Don't you recognize me anymore?'

'Of course not, I'm visited by dozens of Souads here each day! You can't expect me to remember everything!'

'Souad from the women's hair salon, does that ring any bells?'

'Oh, that Souad… Tell me, my child. What can I do for you?'

'Something terrible happened.' I try my best to emphasize the gravity of the situation, it isn't exactly something to be sneezed at after all. It's witchcraft; incredibly dangerous and those who play with it can absolutely destroy you from a distance.

'Well, Beardman. When I came into work this morning there was butter on the floor, I walked right through it. And my working station is covered in henna.'

'Alright, call me back tomorrow.'

'Tomorrow, tomorrow?! I'll be dead meat by then. You can't leave me like this!'

'Sorry, child, but I don't have any time right now.'

'*Wili*, Beardman. Didn't I buy an anti-voodoo amulet for five thousand euros from you a few months ago… does that ring any bells?'

'I guess so.'

'Well, the thing obviously doesn't work! What are you going to do about it?!'

A brief pause at the other end.

'Mister medicine man? Sir…'

'Tell me, what is happening?'

'Well, Hatim, the owner of Lala Rosa, wants to put the business in my name. I suspect my co-worker Layla has something to do with it. Maybe she used voodoo against me, because the salon is most likely in her name. You know?'

'Really?' he utters, clearly surprised as if he has walked straight into some cheap soap series – I wonder if he can still follow me.

'Perhaps it's better you come see me then,' he says, hesitatingly.

'When? What time?'

'As soon as possible, but first you have to arrange something for me.'

'What?' I sigh and bite my lip. That voodoo fear is almost completely gone.

'Do you have pen and paper with you?'

'Yes,' I tell Beardman.

'You will bring a parentless virgin mouse.'

'What?' I ask in astonishment. 'A virgin mouse? I don't know if I can arrange that right this afternoon. Where am I supposed to get such a creature?'

'Take your time and go find your mouse. In the meantime, I'll make sure the magic that has been scattered for you and the voodoo doll they use to make you lose your mind will stop working for now.'

'A voodoo doll? I'm being worked over with a voodoo doll… ouch!! Ouch!!'

'What's wrong, my child?' I can still hear Beardman say on the other end of the line.

'Aiaiai! Ouch! Ouch!'

'Souad, what's wrong? Talk to me!' I hear the medicine man calling breathlessly.

'I don't know what it is, mister Beardman, but it's like my body is being pierced with pins… This isn't right, someone is working on me… Aiaiai! What is this?!'

'Don't you worry child.'

'Are you sure? 'Cause I'm getting the impression that's exactly what I should do.'

'Don't you worry child; I gave you my word.'

'So someone is manipulating me with a voodoo-doll? A voodoo-doll!'

'Yes,' the old blind fortune teller says, 'the world is crazier each day,' he mumbles with a sigh, 'who would do such a thing?'

It's probably that crazy bitch Layla, who else?

'But what am I to do? I have to work in a minute, get it?' I tell him I can't just leave to go look for a mouse.

'Again, don't worry. Everything will be fine.'

Phew, that's just my luck…

I mumble a goodbye and hang up.

I run through all kinds of scenarios for finding a parentless virgin mouse. In the meantime, the salon has filled up again with hordes of customers, busily chatting to each other. And I haven't even mentioned the loud wedding music and blasting blow-dryers yet. A day at Lala Rosa never seemed this long. Every now and then I feel the pins pierce my body. Could it be Layla? I can totally picture her sticking pins into a voodoo-doll.

'Next,' I call randomly at the waiting table, where a group of women is chatting away. Meanwhile, I wipe the locks of hair from my chair with a red duster and put my Jaguar scissors back into my skinny jeans.

F'dila and Dijana are constantly bickering behind me, straight through the music, hurling accusations back and forth. I still wonder how Dijana does it: bickering and cutting her customer's hair into the perfect shape at the same time.

'Those bangs are completely skewed!' I hear Dijana call, followed by:

'*Ah*-mind your own business!'

I'm starting to go bananas, with all this fighting going on. And I keep thinking about this morning's situation. The butter, the henna and the voodoo-doll. It's unbelievable. The atmosphere has turned grim and I'm even considering quitting and looking for a new job… No, that's exactly what the magic wants me to do, this is the voodoo's work! It would be just what Layla wanted.

'Take a seat,' I invite Janice, my faithful regular who comes here for an aubergine dye and to have her split ends cut. The sweat is trickling down my temples and I keep feeling stitches in my body. How the hell am I supposed to find an un-fucked orphan mouse? I can't just call a guy to take care of it, or whatever… What a ridiculous request that would be!

'How are you?' I ask, as I start combing Janice's hair and take a fresh piece of Bubblicious.

'Oh, pretty good,' she tells me, but I have no idea what she's rattling on about. The only things I can think about are the voodoo doll, the sharp pins and the mouse.

'Wow, are you serious,' I say, like I usually do when I don't remember what people are talking about.

'I know, and then...' Janice continues.

'That sucks,' I say without thinking, as I gaze at myself in the mirror for a while. I'm a bit shocked; is this how I always chew my gum? With my jaw sliding sideways instead of going up and down... I look like a cow grinding a bunch of grass for the millionth time!

'And what do *you* think?' Janice suddenly turns her head. Stunned, I keep gazing at her, then shamelessly burp out my answer, like some grunting bovine. 'Moohoooo...'

'Wow, is everything alright?' she asks, worried.

'Excuse me, I drank a little too much Cherry Coke.' Apologetically I cover my mouth with my hand. I should stop drinking coke on an empty stomach early in the morning.

'Well, it won't be long before you throw up all over the place,' Janice adds a little extra, 'You really should see a doctor if you keep burping like this.'

'You know what you're going to do? You're going home, you're sick!' Dijana orders and waves her hand to indicate I can leave.

'You're right, I really am sick... I'm going home.' First, I stick the pointed comb back in my pants and then gloomily catch my tears one by one. They're gliding down my cheeks. How could Layla do this to me? Is she really that heartless? I thought we were friends...

'Don't be dramatic, just go home. People feeling sorry for themselves give me a headache,' Dijana sighs, shaking her head with disapproval.

I park my Fiesta across from Richard Shoes, the store I visited with Hatim this morning. I struggle to stop letting out those weird burps all the time. I really do sound like a cow or a bleating goat. I don't like visiting pet stores; they smell, they are stuffed with creepy animals and most of all I think it's always an unhygienic mess. But I don't have a choice today. After paying for parking, I carefully enter the pet store. I hope they have no animals running around here, such as dogs… Because here's the thing: I'm scared of dogs and cats, they're always tickling your legs, leaving hair everywhere.

'Good afternoon,' I am welcomed by the shop owner, who is wearing an old-fashioned fisherman's sweater.
    'Hey, have you got any mice?' I ask him kindly.
    'I do have rats.'
    'Ugh! Who would buy a rat?' I mumble to myself.
    'Sorry, we don't have any mice here,' the man snaps and smacks his hand on the counter. Then he goes back to the piles of animal food he was unpacking. I walk further into the store, but don't know where to look. There are so many animals and animal things, so I just admire the big aquariums. I do like fish. I might buy one, they're always shiny and cause little inconvenience. It's the perfect pet if you ask me.

Phew, how am I going to get my hands on a virgin orphan mouse? How the hell am I supposed to catch and transport such a creature? I wouldn't even think of laying a finger on it, as I'm afraid of mice, too…
    'And what's that over there?' I ask, surprised, and point at the fat white mice. Those look kind of cute. 'Isn't that a mouse?' I ask the shop owner.
    'Those aren't mice, they're Russian dwarf hamsters.'
    'Is that a kind of mouse?'

'No, they're hamsters.'

'They look like mice.'

'But they're hamsters.'

'But they look like mice, right?' I ask, throwing my hand on my hip.

'Fine. They're like mice.' the owner snaps, and gets back to unpacking his boxes.

Would Beardman notice the difference? Oh well, he's as blind as a bat. He won't be able to tell the difference between a mouse and a hamster. And if you ask me, a Russian dwarf hamster passes as a mouse just fine.

'Let's ask,' I mumble, as I walk towards the shop owner again.

'Yesss,' the owner says, agitatedly.

'These Russian dwarf mice.'

'You mean hamsters,' the man smacks the counter again.

'You know what I mean, *Papi*.'

'Fine, what do you want to know?' the man asks, clearly annoyed.

'Is there a young one between them?'

'They're not that old.'

'And is there one in there without parents?'

The man looks up as if I'm crazy.

'None of those little ones has parents.'

'So, they're orphans?'

The man frowns in surprise. 'Well, if you look at it like that then yes, they are orphans. But if you ask me all animals here are orphans. That stick insect over there is an orphan and the water turtles in the tank, they're also all orphans,' the shop-keeper sighs.

'And did those Russian hamsters have intercourse yet?'

'Miss, I don't know what you're planning on doing with this animal…'

'I just wanna know if… Maybe I'll take two, a male and a female…' I'm making mating moves with my hands.

'Well, I would wait a few weeks. These are really still too young.' the shopkeeper says.

'Okay.' I gaze into the distance for a bit.

'May I take one Russian hamster from you? The white one please.'

'Just the one?'

'Yes, just the one.'

I walk out of the pet store smugly, carrying a plastic bag with an aquarium containing the parentless virgin hamster who is having a wonderful time on a wheel. Outside, the sun is suddenly shining nicely. Ah, I'm glad that has been taken care of, I sigh, standing in front of my parked car. I plan to visit the medicine man straight away. Phew, what a relief, truly a weight off my shoulders. Beardman and his impossible tasks. Couldn't he think of something simpler?

I snatch the car keys out of my shoulder bag and put on my sunglasses. Now that I've bought the mouse, I notice the stitches in my body have stopped. It's as if the anti-voodoo is beginning to work already. I open the door of my car and look at the passenger's seat, which is filled with plastic bags from Richard Shoes. I put the bags in the back seat to make space for my white Russian hamster mouse.

'Souad! Souad!' I suddenly hear behind me. I turn around…

'Baktha! What a coincidence to see you here,' I greet Hatim's wife. What is she doing here? To think I was here this morning, happily shopping with her husband! And the fact the business is soon to be put in my name…

'Eh, ha-ha, hi Baktha!'

'Did you find out more?' Baktha asks, straightforward.

'Yes,' I answer directly. I pull her closer and whisper into her hijab.

'I have a strong feeling Layla is having an affair with your husband. Lala Rosa is in *her* name.'

'*Wili, wili!* Are you serious?!'

'You know what you should do? Visit her father and confront him. I bet he'll make couscous out of her,' I say, and give her a big wink. 'Shall I give you the address?' I ask confidently, and fold my arms with wicked pleasure.

———

CHAPTER 9

Layla

The blind limping chicken

'You may come in, Layla,' the sorcerer says.

I sit down on the grubby sheepskin opposite the blind, wrinkled man. He is wearing a pair of flashy aviator sunglasses. The room is dark, spooky and I don't know where I'd rather be; here, or in the waiting room where the air is even more stuffy. Stuffier than the heavy smell of charcoal and flint that dominates this space.

A cloud of incense penetrates my nose and lungs. Sometimes you just need to push your luck a little, which is why I'm here. But I'm mostly here because I worry my family will find out. I'm dead if my dad figures out Lala Rosa was in my name all along. My parents will think it's a strange and shady story. They will try to find out more and do thorough research. This will automatically lead to Hatim, his wife and his children. Phew, I can't bear to think about it.

'So, this is your first ever consultation with a medicine man?' the old blind man asks, scratching his nose.

'Yes,' I manage hesitantly, 'you could put it like that, yes.' It's not entirely true, because a long time ago, when I was about twelve years old, my aunt took me to see one. I don't remember why exactly, but it was very likely my mother's doing because she wanted to deliver me from the evil eye. The two things my mother fears are: what other people think of you *and* the evil eye.

The medicine man my aunt took me to, happened to be blind as well. He too was ancient, wore glasses and a faded djellaba, and sat on sheepskins. That man communicated via an improvised walkie-talkie. It was a hose with a plastic cup, which went through the wall. This was how he communicated with his wife and son, who also was a blind fortune teller.

I remember how I had to take off all my clothes then, leaving only my underpants. Then he made me stand above an incense burner, with my aunt watching. I felt so embarrassed. It wasn't really clear to me why I had to do that, but it was supposed to be a protective measure.

The medicine man told us to bury a chicken's egg in the grave of a child. The egg in question was supposed to come from a blind, limping chicken. We searched high and low for a sightless chicken with a limp that could lay eggs as well. At the end of the day, we found one with a family who kept chickens and lived just outside town. The chicken was black and henna red and blind on one side; she had once been attacked and scratched by a cat. My aunt and I hurried and took a cab to the cemetery just before dark.

Once we arrived at the cemetery, we wiped away some sand at the first grave we stumbled upon, and that's where my aunt put the egg. Why? I'll be damned if I know.

Since then I've steered clear from all those practices and haven't been involved with any other hocus-pocus. Because all those practices are haram. Even more haram than haram and maybe even more haram than drinking alcohol and eating pork at the same time. Maybe even more haram than smoking weed and wearing a miniskirt that reveals your ass. And yet here I am, like so many others, visiting a fortune teller we refer to as 'a medicine man', as if he's a real doctor. I pray every day, I don't drink alcohol, I don't eat pork and I don't smoke. 'Phew,' I sigh deeply. I'm desperate, I am at a complete loss… Necessity knows no bounds – or rather money plus voodoo knows no bounds.

'What's this trick going to cost me, anyway?' I have a fifty-dollar bill on me and that's all there is. That should cover the costs, right? I think every fortune teller asks for fifty for their consultation.

'Listen, my child, I don't want to talk about money… What's your name?'

'Layla.'

'Layla,' the sorcerer repeats mysteriously.

'And what is your mother's name?'

'Rahma.'

'Very well.' The medicine man is rubbing some stones in his hand.

'Layla, daughter of Rahma,' he says, and then utters some dreadful sounds. They literally give me the chills. He isn't summoning Illuminati ghosts or pontificating on Maya calendars, is he… *Wili, wili,* what am I doing here?

The flames of the candles that were silently burning before, now start to dance wildly. My heart is in my mouth. Damn, this guy is good…

The sorcerer takes a cup and rattles it. Then he hurls the contents onto the floor. The stones, that turn out to be shells, come rolling out of the cup like marbles. Then he picks them up again and repeats the process a few times.

'Where did you say you work again?' the medicine man asks, rattling the cup. It's as if he knew before, but has forgotten about it.

'At Lala Rosa, the hair salon.' I had not told him yet.

'You're Layla!' the sorcerer shrieks and stops rattling, as if he's had a huge fright.

Alarmed, I take a big gulp of air. 'Yes, Layla, daughter of Rahma...'

Then the man begins to snigger loudly, his aviators almost falling off his nose, as his shells tumble onto his lap and onto the concrete floor.

The fortune teller picks up the shells and resumes the rattling of his cup. He is reciting spells now, too. When he's finished, he takes a deep bow and offers his gratitude, like the Chinese do, to something that appears to be standing behind me. I turn around, but see nothing, nada, nix.

'Layla, Layla, Layla,' the man mumbles, worried.

Am I in such deep trouble? Now I'm really starting to worry.

'You have many enemies at the moment,' he says, placing his finger on a few shells, as if he is reading them like that. I shake my head in incomprehension.

'Why? I never hurt anybody.' What enemies am I supposed to have?

'Everything, absolutely everything is about Lala Rosa.'

'Really?' I sigh deeply and begin to tell my story, desperate for someone to lighten my load. Because that's why I'm here: my future.

'You see, a few years ago I was in a relationship with a man. Then I discovered he was married, so I ended our affair. His hair salon for ladies was already in my name and I kept it like that. In exchange I was able to work there, received decent pay, and this man still pays for my education.

Now I want to get out of this deal, but he is harassing me, or rather tormenting me with a lot of hassle. Nobody, and I mean nobody, knows the salon is in my name. Everyone thinks it's in his wife's name, and if my parents find out… I'm dead.'

'I believe you have bigger problems to worry about right now, my child.'

'Oh?' I frown in surprise, what is this man talking about anyway? 'What kind of problems?'

'You have enemies, lots of enemies at the moment.' The man snatches the shells from the ground, rattles them and throws them out on the floor again.

'Particularly your co-workers, I see.'

What exactly is he seeing, I thought he was blind?

'What exactly are you seeing?' I ask, curiously. What enemies am I supposed to have at work? Dijana is a sweetheart and Souad and I are kind of friends. F'dila, I don't even know that woman… I really wouldn't know.

'I see the hair salon is in high demand.' The fortune teller picks his shells up from the ground. 'The proceeds are high and there are customers at all times.'

I'm beginning to suspect I'm wasting my time here. Maybe I should just hand him my fifty euros and leave. I can't even feel my behind on this trashy sheep skin, it tingles on all sides. I think this sorcerer is a creep and his prophecies are crap. I've been here half an hour and he hasn't uttered a word of sense yet.

'I see a Souad,' the fortune teller suddenly says. 'And a certain F'dila… Is that right?'

'What… what are you saying?!' My nostrils spread like the wings of a young falcon learning to fly, jumping off a cliff for the first time. 'Souad?' I repeat with some surprise. 'And F'dila?'

'You are in great danger, my child. It's a good thing that you came to see me,' the sorcerer says as he picks some shells up from the concrete, leaving the others where they are.

'What kind of danger?' I shout as I slap my hands on my thighs, '*Wili,* you can't be serious! First Hatim and now Souad and F'dila, what do they want from me?'

'Everyone wants the hair salon and everyone is jealous. But together you and I are going to put a stop to that.' The medicine man drops the shells into the cup, one by one.

'But, what exactly did they do? Something in my food, did I eat something? I have had some trouble focusing on my thesis recently. Is it witchcraft? Tell me! Did they sneak something in my food, so I wouldn't be able to write my thesis?'

'Yes.'

'Those dirty bitches!'

'Don't worry. What you do have to worry about is the voodoo that's being scattered all over the salon right now. If that F'dila cannot get her hands on Hatim and the salon, she is determined to destroy everyone.' The sorcerer is waving his wooden cup.

'What about Souad? What's her part in this story?' I suddenly hear myself asking.

'She wants to get her hands on the salon, too. She is determined to become the owner. She's busy trying to win over Hatim and he is very close to putting the business in her name… But isn't that what you wanted? You want to get rid of Lala

Rosa, right?' He is now playing with his beard, waiting for my answer.

There's a silence. I look around, a little dazed.

'What is it going to be, my child? Will you let everyone walk all over you?' the medicine man breaks the silence.

I'm torn… I did want to get rid of Lala Rosa, and from what I'm hearing that is not a problem anymore. But now that I know Souad and F'dila are preying on the salon too, I'm less certain I want to let it go. Lala Rosa might still be too precious to me and maybe it's high time I step forward as its owner. Why didn't I do that a long time ago? My parents would probably have been proud of me if they knew I had my own business. That makes me a real business woman, one with a lawyer's office in the pipeline, too. I just don't know; do I want to get rid of Lala Rosa?

'Hatim is the key to your problem and you know it.' The sorcerer throws the shells out on the floor again.

'But what am I supposed to do?' I ask him desperately.

'I see, you still love him. Look.' The man points at a few shells, lying on the floor in the shape of a heart. I still love Hatim…

'And he still loves you, too. Maybe you should sleep on it? You know what, come back again next week. When you've thought it through and you know what you want; the hair salon, Hatim… I think that's the best solution for now.'

'But what about the voodoo they're using against me now?'

'I'll give you some *bgor*, they are incense stones you have to burn completely. You take off all your clothes and really let the smoke work itself into you. You can also do it here, if you want,' the medicine man offers.

'And then take off my clothes right here?'
'Yes. I'm blind anyway, my child.'
'I'd prefer doing it at home. What do I owe you?'

'Today we do not speak of money, we'll talk about it next time.'

CHAPTER 10

F'dila

The voodoo doll

The doll is the spitting image of Souad. I have to say the healer really has done an excellent job. The tiger print fabric covering this heap of straw... everything is Souad. To avoid any mix-ups and just to make the difference between Souad and myself very, very clear, I'm wearing a wide skirt, pajama pants and a neatly fringed blouse on top. The outfit is completed by the orange apron with the white embroidered flowers. 'Ah-F'dila! You seem to have rolled off the mountain, you farm girl! What kind of combination is that?' was Boubker's comment this morning.

Souad's voodoo doll has a head and a torso. The eyes are painted with charcoal and the mouth with non-kosher blood from some animal the sorcerer sacrificed to the spirits. The voodoo doll also has Souad's hair: the split ends I collected and gave to the doctor during my first consultation. The locks were long enough to be used for the doll. Souad always cuts her split ends, even when she doesn't have them.

The healer and I had named the voodoo doll Souad. He told me to take the doll in my left hand, upon which I was to speak the following words: 'From now on, you shall be called Souad.' Then he lit a white candle and took seven pins. He held the pins in the flame of the white candle until the heat discolored them. After this ritual I was allowed to poke the voodoo doll with the pins one by one. Whenever I want something bad to happen to Souad, I pull a needle and jam it into the doll.

While stabbing, I utter all my most serious curses at Souad, 'Fall apart, bitch!' 'Drop down, whore!'

When no one notices, I walk to Lala Rosa's kitchen and quickly poke the doll with a few pins. I have no work to do anyway. 'I hate you bitch!' slips out of my mouth just a little too loudly. 'You're possessed by a cow, you stupid bitch!' I say, stabbing the doll as hard as I can. Somehow, with each puncture, I feel relieved and liberated… 'Quit your job at Lala Rosa,' and I stick the needle right through her heart. And, 'I want you to crumble like old concrete.' Then I take another little needle, 'Get migraines until you drop, you slut!'

I feel powerful. I feel invincible with my Souad voodoo doll, the pins and the fire letter the doctor gave me for Hatim and his wife. Tonight, when Boubker is on his night shift, I will burn the fire letter with an incense burner. Simultaneously, according to the sorcerer's instructions, I must speak my curses to Baktha and express my wishes for Hatim, seven times each.

Within a week, the healer assured me, my wishes will come true. It won't be long before the marriage between Baktha and Hatim is over and he will put a ring on my finger. The doctor has also given me a powder for Hatim. I have to mix that into a glass of alcohol and make him drink it. I just have to figure out how to go about this. Hatim doesn't drink alcohol, or does he? The sorcerer was very clear: Hatim really must drink the powder mixed with alcohol. And from then on it will be left when I say left, and right when I say right. Oh well, necessity knows no bounds…

From now on I can hurt anyone if I want to. Especially now that the healer has shown me how to make a voodoo doll for someone. Maybe I'll make one for Boubker too. Boubker has been a little too sassy lately. Perhaps I'll make one for Jaap as well, so he will stop visiting Boubker. I hate Jaap... and Boubker. Actually, I hate everyone. For a second my mind drifts to Mrs Professor. I would have loved to make her a voodoo doll too. Shame I don't have a lock of hair from that woman. I regret not keeping some of that sanitary towel. Next time I will approach things differently and from now on I will always save something for later.

My main target now is Lala Rosa. The business must be put in my name as soon as possible and Hatim must make sure there is an unforgettable wedding. Everything will work out with the voodoo that the healer has given me. My only concern is how to pay for all of this. I don't actually have those five thousand euros to pay him. Oh well. Everything is more than worth it.

'It's about time she got a hair dryer and start doing something,' Dijana grumbles. No matter how loud the music is, I can clearly hear her from the kitchen. Today it's just Dijana and me working at Lala Rosa. Souad called in sick yesterday. See, this proves the voodoo doll has done its job and, in my hands, will continue to do so for a very long time. Layla never works on Tuesdays. According to the customers' gossip, the stupid chick is still at school. Trust me, no school can teach her what I know and that is a very good thing... I see no threat in Layla, the stupid cow. Hatim dislikes her too, I noticed. The deadly looks he gives her all the time speak volumes.

I decide to tuck the voodoo doll into my apron. At that exact moment, Dijana calls me, 'F'dila, customer!'

While the music is buzzing loudly from the speakers and Dijana is busy epilating, the old woman in the green djellaba and her friend in the orange djellaba are jabbering to each other. They're enjoying the cup of 'free' coffee they come to get here each day. In between, they leaf through Vogue magazine and the XL edition of Elle. As I prep my work zone for my very first client, Selma, I can't help but eavesdrop on the two lisping ladies, the orange and green djellaba.

'So you exercise Pilates, girl? If I may honestly tell you, it doesn't really show, sister. Are you sure you're not just imagining it?'

'Doesn't show? I do Pilates every Wednesday afternoon. I also recently learned to ride a bicycle. Can you cycle?'

'Cycling, me? Of course not… I have my son, so I don't have to cycle. My son takes me everywhere I want. Even if I were to call my son in the middle of the night, he would be right there waiting for me with his car. Even if he were on holiday in a faraway country, he would come rushing to me like a real gentleman. My son would leave his family just for me and only me. He'd pick me up in his new Audi 45, which he just bought. It is this year's model. And the rims still shine like finely cut diamonds.'

'My son has a Mercedes Land Rover 55, it's a new kind of model. It even has a built-in satellite TV.'

'No, no. My son wouldn't bother with satellite TV in his car. But what he does have is a pilot license. Next year my son will personally fly us to Tangier for a vacation. Then you go and watch satellite TV in that Mercedes Land Rover.'

'Well, we'll be waiting for you to fly away forever… Would you look at this! No one would call this coffee, would they?'

If only I had a man with a satellite TV in his car or a pilots' license, I suddenly realize. Now that would impress my village. And as for the coffee, the ladies are right, it doesn't taste of anything. This entire salon lacks taste!

Just wait until I'm in charge here. I'll change everything in an instant.

My customer is chatting to Dijana. I can't quite hear what they are talking about. The woman in question is still young and is wearing very smart clothes. She reminds me of Mrs Professor. She has the same nauseating presence… Instantly the hairs in my neck stand on end like clipped blades of grass. The woman in question is wearing a pencil skirt, a jacket and high boots, which give the impression that they are very expensive. She is holding a briefcase in her hand.

'Come here,' I beckon the woman towards me. A customer at long last!

I can breathe a sigh of relief, because for a moment it seemed I was in the salon for nothing. Since the epilation incident, I have done nothing but sweep the floor and waste time daydreaming. Rumors about the epilation drama spread like wildfire and now no customer dares to subject themselves to my hairdressing skills.

'Good morning,' the woman greets me with a smile. A wave of sweet perfume hits me. I wonder what brand this is? It's probably very expensive. The lady looks refined, modest and also charming in a very classic way. A typical professor type. I don't like her at all – yuck – with her posh haircut! Who does that cow think she is? Aah-go buy a pack of underpants at Primark! That's how it goes with these types of people, they look slick on the outside, but underneath those clothes you will find nothing but sticky, dirty underpants. The bitch!

'You have nice hair,' I tell the troll with her bob line haircut. The woman sits down in the chair and casually throws her briefcase on the floor. What would be in there? Money? Important paperwork? Well, I'd rather shove it down her throat. The woman in question is inspecting my outfit in the mirror in an unpleasant way. What, what? Does she have a problem with me? As if she's so good looking… All those other women who come here are at least wearing Burberry and Dolce & Gabanna. What is she wearing? Nothing, no brand whatsoever…

'How would you like your hair done?' I ask the professor type lady.

'Just the split ends,' the woman's reflection says, 'and blow dry, please.'

'OK,' I repeat her words: 'Split ends and blow-dry.' Even though I've never cut a wisp of hair in my life… Operating the blow dryer doesn't seem too complicated. There is a first time for everything. From the cart I take a pair of colorful scissors with a Jaguar logo. I put the Jaguar scissors between my fingers. At least it looks interesting! And really, how hard can it be?

I feverishly put a strand of dry hair between my fingers and focus on the Jaguar scissors making their debut. The first cuts go smoothly and before I know it, a flurry of hair locks is falling down. 'Not too short, please' the professor type lady reminds me. Meanwhile, she is chatting to Dijana. The two are gossiping about Mona, who has been drugged by her ex-in-laws and transported back to her hometown. As the tufts of hair fall down like swirling autumn leaves, I listen attentively to Mona's story.

Minutes pass and I am starting to sweat. With a seemingly professional look, I appraise the posh lady's hair. Somehow, I don't seem to be able to 'straighten things out'. I also realize that her haircut has been shortened a bit too much. That will have to be the Jaguar scissors. What a small pair of scissors.

You can't cut properly with those, can you? I decide it's time to trade in the Jaguar scissors for the big red fabric scissors, which I bought at the supermarket this weekend. I lift the tool out of the front pocket of my apron and put the Jaguar scissors down on the barber's table.

I ruffle firmly through the hair of the professor type lady, the wisps that have been cut this way and that are more visible now. Then, I have no idea why, I start massaging her scalp. 'Ah, this feels really good,' says the lady, still chatting away with Dijana about all sorts of things. Dijana herself seems to have no problem talking, sweating like a pig and epilating at the same time.

Then I pull the professor type lady's hair together to cut off a nice straight piece in one go. Just to get her bob line all at same length. Those large scissors will be like a hot knife through butter.

'Are you almost done?' My customer now asks hurriedly, checking her watch. 'Because I have to go back to court in a minute.' 'Oh yes,' I say to the professor type lady. One more cut and then I can start blow drying.

I have to be quick, because the lady 'still has to go to court'. I no longer hesitate. I close my eyes… and then the locks of hair fly around. Like a cat that has mercilessly fallen into an icy ditch, Mrs Lawyer jumps out of her chair… Meanwhile, I examine the haircut which I think looks pretty good. I have to say, those supermarket scissors have done an excellent job.

In absolute shock, Mrs Lawyer turns around and fills the salon with her screaming. It's always the same with these kinds of cows…

CHAPTER 11

Souad

It's all about status

The virgin orphan mouse is running at nearly the speed of light in the wheel in his hamster cage. I have given it a prominent place in the living room – on the black dresser, to be precise. I wonder what my mom will say when she gets home from work: 'What is this *ah*-Souad?!'

When it comes to mice, my mother is a real scaredy-cat. She can scream everyone's head off. To make things easy I have named the mouse Gorbachev. He's from Russia after all. I don't know what that medicine man intends to do with the little creature. Would gory violence be part of the anti-voodoo ritual?

My thoughts are spinning in rhythm with the running wheel. Gorbachev can't get enough of it. I stare angrily at the rodent… Those bitches have worked me over with spells and a voodoo doll! What are they planning on doing with me? I can feel them, I can feel their hate. How they must be working their incense burners and commanding all their hocus-pocus-controlled ghosts to chase me. I can feel it in the hairs on my neck, which are on end at all times. I can feel it in my bones. I can just feel they are trying to make me lose my mind. I feel it in my aching head and my tired legs. I must do something to protect myself! I clench my teeth bitterly.

Determinedly, I stare at the creature, clumsily speeding in his wheel. The cage is filled with innocence, pouring out of the little runner. I will make them pay… one by one! But what will Beardman do with my hamster-mouse later?

The living room is quiet. All you can hear is the spinning wheel squeaking.

Then there's no more doubt… I get up and walk towards the cage. Gorbachev is anxiously looking at my acrylic nails, stalking him like ruthless knives. He flounders, but doesn't stand a chance. I have no choice. The mouse must die.

The blind medicine man takes his place on one of the sheepskins. I pull the mouse out of the large Richard Shoes bag. I brought some hamster food in case he gets hungry.

As soon as I scatter some of it into the palm of my hand, the mouse starts kicking the air with his short little paws. Gorbachev's appetite really reminds me of my own. I'm always hungry too. I could really go for a shrimp-filled *bara* at the moment. And the mouse is a big fan of energy drinks, just like I am. I filled his water bottle with a few drops of the drink this afternoon. He couldn't get enough of it.

I stroke Gorbachev's velvet fur with my fingertips, while he is nibbling his food.

'Well, well,' Beardman sighs. Then he starts shaking his cup of shells, as if he's playing with a rattle. I can barely keep myself from laughing. It really looks ridiculous, the way he is sitting there.

'Did you bring your mouse?' the man asks, rattling away in the meantime.

First, I giggle and tickle Gorbachev with my acrylic nails. Then I answer him, 'yes, here's your virgin orphan mouse, just as you requested.'

'How wonderful,' says the medicine man and he instantly stops rattling.

'He comes all the way from Russia,' I tell him.

'Really?' he says, firmly rubbing his head, 'all the way from Russia, you little devil.' He laughs out loud and his cup falls out of his hands and into his lap.

'*Wili*, Beardman? What did you think? You wanted a virgin orphan mouse, right? Well, then I'll get you one.' I give the blind man a wink. If he would have asked me for an elderly turtle with an IQ of 164, I would have gotten him one of those too.

Meanwhile, Gorbachev rushes from my shoulder to the palm of my hand. There he starts munching his hamster food again. Even though I have a lot on my mind now with the spells and the voodoo doll and the whole shebang, Gorbachev's company makes me feel giddy rather than worried.

'Alright, let's begin,' Beardman gathers his shells again.

'What about the voodoo doll? Has it stopped now? Was it Layla?' I ask, deeply concerned.

'That I have almost completely taken care of,' he tells me, reassuringly. I sigh a breath of relief.

'But,' he suddenly starts, 'you must not trust anyone. You have only enemies at Lala Rosa. They would like nothing better than to destroy you. At the moment they're even…' he says, but I interrupt him before he can finish his sentence: 'What do they want from me? What have I done to hurt them?' The man hesitates, as if he has to pick his words off the concrete, the way he does with his shells.

There's silence.

'It is really simple Souad,' the medicine man breaks the silence, 'everyone has set their sights on Lala Rosa. And Hatim has his focus on you,' the man giggles. 'Now do you understand what is going on?'

'Yes, is there any man who is *not* focused on me?' I tell Beard-man, 'of course Hatim has set his sights on me, too.' Then my thoughts wander to Layla. I'll turn that bitch into shish kebab! The medicine man resumes his rattling. A minute later, the shells scatter on the concrete with a loud noise. Gorbachev climbs back to my shoulder from the palm of my hand.

'It's F'dila,' Beardman suddenly says.

'What?' I ask him, confused.

'Here, look,' the man says, pointing at his scattered shells.

'Do you see it?' he asks, but I shake my head.

'Take a close look. It's F'dila, not Layla.'

The man is mistaken, I'm sure.

'Well, this is getting really weird,' I sigh and shake my head. Then I put Gorbachev back onto my lap. 'Seriously, I'll beat everyone to a pulp!' I grunt with clenched fists.

'Keep calm!' Beardman warns me, 'we will go about this differently. They focus on their work and you focus on yours. We will tackle this together without anyone knowing about it. And in the meantime, those ladies will not be able to hurt you.'

'Okay,' I fold my arms pensively. He is right in some way. If they don't know what's going on, I might get far more out of it. 'You tell me, because honestly, I don't understand a thing anymore.'

'You tell *me*, Souad. What do *you* want? Lala Rosa? Hatim?'

'I want Lala Rosa, for sure. I want that place to be all mine. And I want that voodoo shit to stop. That is what I want.'

'So you have set your mind on the salon and nothing but the salon?' Beardman asks me.

'Totally, totally,' I tell him.

'Alright.' The man starts rattling his shells again. 'Let's first do something about that witchcraft they are doing for you. I will give you a fire letter later, which will ensure the salon is put entirely in your name. And Hatim? Do I need to give you something for Hatim, too?'

'Why?' I ask the ancient fortune teller in confusion.

'To make Hatim fall for *you*?'

'*Wili*, Beardman, have you lost your mind? I can have any man I want. Why would I choose that crackerhead? The only things I want from Hatim are his money and the salon.' I tell him. Beardman starts giggling.
I don't want a man at all. I want expensive shoes and bags and I want to be seen in the fancy parts of town.

The medicine man puts all the shells back into the rattle. Sometimes it's like all he ever does is rattle, rattle, rattle. Meanwhile I keep asking myself what I'm doing here. 'Phew!' I'm tired, hungry and I have a headache.
I don't know how he does it, the man is blind as a bat and still manages to pile up and light the charcoal with smooth, almost seductive, movements. All at once he begins to recite all kinds of spells as he blows into the old-fashioned incense burner. I thought I'd come in and quickly have that voodoo removed. But before you know it, three hours have passed. It's like Lala Rosa.
He drops the incense stones on the smoldering charcoal one by one…
'Quick, give me the mouse!' Beardman suddenly orders breathlessly.
'Right!' I call without thinking as I lift the shy little thing

from my lap and put it in his dry hands. A big plume of smoke is just escaping from the burner. It really bothers Gorbachev, the poor thing…

'Is this even a mouse?' He feels Gorbachev with his fingers.

'Yes, of course,' I say, determined, 'It's a Russian mouse, they have shorter tails,' I explain.

'I see,' he says, dangling Gorbachev from left to right above the incense burner. The mouse begins to panic and squeaks and fights the plumes around him with his little paws. It's horrible to watch, but I have to. I don't have a choice.

'It will be over in a second,' I tell Gorbachev. Meanwhile Beardman says things in a language I'm unable to understand. Then he pulls out a knife from under the sheepskin. It's blunt and made out of brass with signs and figures engraved into it. The dark spells are flowing out of his mouth with greater speed and the knife comes closer and closer. What does he plan to do with it? '*Wili, wili!* What are you doing?' I shout.

'We are removing the voodoo, aren't we?' Beardman quickly hides the mouse behind his back. In his other hand he is still holding the knife.

'Can I have my mouse back, please?' I ask very politely. 'Please,' I beg him.

'Do you want to remove the voodoo or not?'

'Can I first have my mouse back, Beardman.'

'Here's your mouse!' He flings the creature into my lap. I sigh a breath of relief; my hamster mouse was close to being dead.

The medicine man clears away the shells and the knife and puts the incense burner aside.

'We were going to take care of everything, but you don't want to,' the old man mumbles grimly. In the meantime, I put the

Russian dwarf mouse and the hamster food back in my bag.

'I can't hurt Gorbachev!' I tell him.

'You want Lala Rosa in your name, right? And you must protect yourself against the voodoo because they are destroying you! Without my protection you won't get anywhere, mark my words!' the man says furiously. His spit is flying all over the place.

Maybe the man is right, and I won't get anywhere without his anti-witchcraft measures. But there is one thing I am sure of: 'this is just wrong!' I say as mad as a hornet. I get up and take a few steps towards the door. I don't know what to do about the hocus-pocus and my plans for Lala Rosa. But I know one thing for certain; I will not hurt Gorbachev.

After aimlessly driving around town for hours and eating a spicy chicken wrap at the halal KFC drive-thru, I drive to the quay by the harbor. I park in the first empty spot I see and put Gorbachev in the pocket of my cardigan, like a worried mother mouse. He's nice and warm in there. I get out and take a seat on the wooden bench at the waterside. It's drizzling. I take a last sip of my coke and shamelessly fling the empty cup underneath the bench. My fingers automatically slide into my cardigan's pocket. I stroke Gorbachev's soft fur, which somehow comforts me.

'It's all about status, you know,' I tell Gorbachev. I pull the mouse out of my pocket. And even though they are no more than tiny black buttons, I look deep into his eyes. Would he feel and understand me? Is he looking at me too?

'It's all about money,' I mumble to myself, 'the club is where you always find men with a lot of money.' I wipe the raindrops off my forehead and decide to keep the mouse in my hands to shield it from the rain.

'What I would like most of all is to be a trophy wife and live in a villa,' I continue. All the while, the mouse is very quiet, as if he's encouraging me to keep talking. 'I want a lot of money and I want to outshine all my friends and family… I want to outshine everyone who keeps treating me as inferior.' I sigh deeply.

CHAPTER 12

Layla

Playing with fire

'Layla, are you okay?' Tee asks.

'Eh, sure…' I say, but I'm too distracted by what is happening behind me.

'What, what! They look pretty, don't they?' F'dila howls. Oh, no… what is it this time?

'*Wili, wili!* My eyebrows!'

I turn around, the smoldering blow dryer still in my hand, and see Dahbia jumping out of F'dila's chair. What was Dahbia even doing there? Everyone knows to stay clear of F'dila, don't they?

'What's she going to do?' Tee asks me. She slaps the giant mop of curls, which I had just parted neatly, out of her face.

Dahbia gets up and ruthlessly pushes F'dila over.

'I would have done the exact same thing,' Tee says to me.

Dijana joins them, but I'm going to stay out of this… When it comes to fighting, I'm a first-class chicken.

'What's going on here?' Dijana asks.

'F'dila, sit down for a minute,' Tee orders her, but F'dila stares at her with a defiant whaddayawant-attitude. Tee decides to keep her mouth shut and I don't blame her. When it comes to F'dila, it's the same as with Olfa, the one with the tattoo leggings who's always fooling around with Hatim. You never know who they are: the mafioso's sister, the mafioso's cousin, the mafioso's wife, the mafioso's lover or the mafioso herself. But a reprisal from the mafia is not what I'm afraid of. What I *am* afraid of is F'dila herself. People like her, with their aprons and saffron smudges on their blouses, can summon some sort of rabies within themselves, along with all other kinds of hostile symptoms common to animals. Perhaps it's because fighting with their cat claws is what they've done their whole lives. This kind of women can easily beat a world boxing champion in a K-1 fight when you cross them.

Then F'dila turns to Dahbia, whose eyebrows she has just ruined completely. I thought we all agreed F'dila wouldn't epilate anymore?

'You whore!' F'dila provokes Dahbia, who is checking her eyebrows in the mirror.

'Don't you dare!' Dijana yells, but it's too late already. F'dila attacks Dahbia with a firm push, Dahbia falls over the hairdresser's chair and crashes down on the floor. F'dila wants to jump on top of her, but Dijana is just in time to grab her by the collar of her blouse.

'Ughhhh,' F'dila turns around and gives Dijana a big punch in the neck.

'Oh, no… a fight!' I cry, completely at a loss. Angry as a gorilla who is being challenged, Dijana grabs her blow dryer and uses it to firmly smack F'dila. F'dila counters and scratches with her nails like a cat gone wild.

'Shit, she's strong,' I can hear Tee say.

I'm standing there watching, static as an antenna. Frozen with fear… I've never dealt well with fighting.

'*Ah*-whore!' F'dila roars.

'Get out, before I smash this blow dryer on your head!' Dijana screams, her face as red as a lobster.

'You just wait, I will get Boubker, my boyfriend, he will turn you into shawarma!' F'dila yells through the salon. Everyone is scared and no one dares to look her in the eye. She picks her hijab up from the floor and stomps towards the coat rack.

'I'm getting my boyfriend!' she roars on the doorstep, 'he is going to finish all of you!'

At least the fighting stopped... Seriously, I'm putting a full claim on Lala Rosa, I decide with a deep sigh. From now on everything has to change, because we really can't go on like this.

'Your face, man, look at that!'

'This is outrageous!'

'Maybe you should see a doctor?'

'You should at least go to the police.'

'Call your GP.'

'You must report it to the police!'

'Do you want me to come to the police station?'

Dijana has deep scratches in her face. They are red, swollen, and I fear they will become permanent scars.

'This is it, I can't do it anymore,' Dijana says, despondently. I want to stop her, but she won't let me come near.

'Stay there,' she tells us. Powerless, I watch how she puts the blow dryer back in its holder and grabs her raincoat from the rack.

'I quit.'

In my bedroom I gloomily take off my clothes and put on my white satin negligee, which even has fake fur on it. I failed...

I lost Dijana, Lala Rosa lost Dijana. No one can epilate as well as Dijana, she's irreplaceable. How did it get to this? Tomorrow or the day after I'll visit the medicine man, for Lala Rosa. All of this is my fault.

Quietly I set fire to the incense in the small earthenware incense bowl. I don't want my parents to notice, so I open the window and lock the door to be safe. I light a match and put it in the bowl. Then I place the brittle blocks of charcoal on top of each other one by one, and blow softly to fan the fire.

As soon as the fire starts crackling, I slowly let the negligee slide off my naked body.

As I'm spreading my legs wide above the smoldering bowl of charcoal, I drop the small incense stones into the burner. Exactly like the old blind sorcerer told me to.

The doorbell rings, I hope it's not for me.

The smoke spreads in all directions, as if my bedroom is on fire. Luckily my window is open, so the smoke can escape. I can hear my father roaring from his window, but I can't tell exactly what he's saying. Maybe it's a Jehovah's Witness, or some rascals playing ring and run. That usually makes my dad vicious.

While I toss the final incense stones on the burner, I hear the argument between my dad and the person at the door getting more intense. Meanwhile the smoke is getting more intense too… What did the medicine man give me? My room is black with smoke by now.

'Layla, what is happening?' my sister bangs loudly on the door. I want to answer her, but I can hardly breathe. Apart from some coughing nothing is coming out of my throat. I

want to walk towards the window for a gulp of fresh air, but
realize just in time that I'm naked.

I hear my father screaming and arguing, and I hear a lady's
voice shouting too… She screams upward, 'your daughter is
a whore!'

I can barely breathe, my father is raging… *Wili, wili,* who is
that woman saying I'm a whore? Help, I can't breathe!

'Do you hear me! You asshole! Your daughter is a whore!'

Wili, wili… it's the wife of Hatim, the rat! My father… *wili,
wili!* I hear my father yelling that the woman has to piss off
and to make things even worse the fire alarm is now also going off.

'Layla, *ah*-idiot, get out of your room! Fire! You have been
playing with fire!'

CHAPTER 13

F'dila

Failure is not an option

Once I'm sure no one sees me, I take the voodoo doll from the pocket of my apron. I put the doll on the counter and examine each pin sticking out of the torso. To avoid attention, I switch on the Senseo machine and fill a dirty cup with coffee. Everyone in the salon is too busy gossiping anyway. No one knows what I'm up to…

I look at the rags that are supposed to be a voodoo doll. The tiger print fabric the doll is dressed in, has large holes in it now. Last night I went a bit too far with a little kitchen knife. When I heard Souad was feeling better, I was boiling with rage. Boubker walked in on me molesting the voodoo doll.

He said: 'What are you doing there, crazy cow.'

To which I replied, '*Ah*-go away, you! I'm making a birthday present for a small girl at work.'

'*Ah*-woman,' Boubker added, 'such a creepy doll will scare the hell out of her.'

'Don't you interfere in women's business.' I replied. Then I kicked him out of the kitchen.

Now the voodoo doll is practically ruined and if I don't handle it with care, Souad will fall apart and I can no longer torture her. One by one I pull out the pins, and then slowly put them back into the body. I'm pricking two pins in her gut so the bitch will never be able to have children. And two pins go straight through Souad's pupils, so the cow will go blind. And finally, I put a few more pins in her head, 'I hate you, bitch! I hate you!'

'Say…
   What are you doing there?'

Oops…

'What is that?' Souad's high heels glide over the faded and sticky kitchen tiles. She looks as if she has just seen a ghost. She holds still, does not go away and stares at me with a look of horror and disgust. Does she know what I'm doing?

I take the voodoo doll from the counter and put it in my apron as quickly as I can. Surely Souad hasn't seen it. And even if she had, she wouldn't be able to make anything of it. The thing pretty much fell apart, so why should I even worry about it. I stare at Souad and want to slip the voodoo doll into my apron without her noticing, but then suddenly she yells 'Give me that!' Souad runs into the kitchen and rips the doll from my hands. Then comes her fleshy fist. It lands in my stomach with a firm punch. 'Ooff!' Pain is shooting in all directions and I can feel the contents of my stomach sloshing. I gasp, the pain rushing through my body is intense. I can vaguely hear Souad walk back into the salon, still clutching the doll in her hands. What is she going to do with it? But I can't think anymore, everything turns black before my eyes.

'*Wili, wili,* that witch has made me a voodoo doll!' I hear her scream in the background.

Now, much to my annoyance, she has also informed all the customers. How could this happen? I'm done for! But due to the stabbing pain in my stomach, I can barely think.

'Would you look at this! Beardman was right after all!' I hear Souad call again.
  'Which Beardman?'
  'Have you gone to see the bearded man?'
  'What? No… Look here, see, a voodoo doll! The doll looks just like me!'

I gasp for breath, defeated and not knowing what to do. This is much worse than the epilation drama with Dahbia and all the awful haircuts put together. And the worst is: what will Hatim think? With great effort I push away the pain in my stomach, the dizziness and all the spots and stars looming before my eyes… I must call Hatim, whatever happens, I must be quicker than Souad and tell him she beat me up. Everyone here treats me like rubbish, just like Mrs Professor did. Like a slave. That's what I am to them: a slave!

There is a lot of commotion in the salon, even the music is turned off. Then one by one I hear them speak evil of me, of how scary I am and how I am not to be trusted… I have to hear how all those whores mercilessly spit yellow and black bile all over me. I would like nothing better than to scratch open their faces one by one, but I don't have the energy for it. The punch Souad just dealt me has almost knocked me out completely. I take my phone out of my apron and search for Hatim's number as quickly as I can. To no avail, Hatim is not answering… I cannot reach him! At the same time I hear that whore in the salon speak to him: 'Hatim, you really must come! *Wili*, what I found here on that F'dila. We really have trouble at work now!'

That bitch Souad has beaten me to it! I am so upset my heart almost jumps out of my windpipe. Now what? What do I do? I quickly smooth out my blouse and straighten my headscarf and skirt. I wrap my apron tight, so it looks nice again. Then I cry as much as I can, so that Hatim will soon see how red and thick my eyes have become. And I sob, very loud and very deep, hoping the customers will also come here to comfort me, to hear what happened and to form an alliance against Souad… But instead, no one comes at all. In fact, the salon empties and I can just hear the old woman in the green djellaba leaving for the first time before closing. 'It's getting crazier here all the time, I'm going home.' I nimbly tiptoe over to the kitchen door to peek into the salon. I just have to know what's going on there… The annoying journalist with the holes in her turtleneck gets up too. 'I guess I'll come back tomorrow then.'

'Sorry, but I really can't do anything right now… Honestly, my hands are shaking… That bitch made me a fucking voodoo doll. A fucking voodoo doll with pins in my head! No wonder I've been having constant headaches! I've had an inexplicable fucking migraine for days!' Souad cries. Much to my annoyance, she is blowing things up. If I could, I would stick a sock in that big mouth of hers and push it down her throat. That bitch just doesn't know when to stop. Souad continues 'She has chased away Dijana too. No one has ever resigned from Lala Rosa before! That witch will be the end of the salon. Mark my words!' Phew, I sigh.

I am just going to stay where I am in the kitchen and wait for Hatim.

Moments later, the last customers have trickled out of Lala Rosa. We are alone in the salon now. Souad and me.

I was convinced Souad would come beat me up as soon as the customers had left. But contrary to my expectations, she sits quietly, waiting. I hear the annoying squeak of the swivel chair Souad is turning around in. She doesn't notice that I'm looking at her, the bitch. So I stand here in the kitchen, motionless.

A second fight with Souad could have worked to my advantage with Hatim even though Souad is very big and sturdy and she has those ice picks that are supposed to be nails. Hatim would have to see she is out of control. That punch she just gave me… I saw stars and planets before my eyes… In the meantime, I do my best to collect my thoughts. What am I to say to Hatim later, so he will stand by my side and fire Souad? My plans must not fail… I have come this far…

CHAPTER 14

Souad

The witch

It's not easy to wipe the astonishment off my face. As soon as I place Gorbachev the hamster-mouse on the mirror table, he scurries towards the pot of Kérastase. He is now part of the mess that's on the table. The creature sticks his nose directly into the pot.

Beardman, that old blind sock, was right after all. It was F'dila, that hypocritical witch! Look at that, a voodoo doll of all things. A real voodoo doll, tailor-made to destroy me! How could I have been so blind?

Have I been too rude and mean to Layla, maybe? Oh, I've made a huge mistake…

I pull my cell phone out of my tiger leggings. I quickly scroll through the device, searching for Baktha's number. I hope she hasn't visited Layla's parents yet, or worse: made a scene at their house. What an embarrassment that must have been… What will I tell that woman anyway?

'Yes!' Baktha shouts through the phone breathlessly. You can hear noisy children in the background.

'Hello,' I say timidly, 'it's Souad.'

'Souad.' That's all I get from Baktha. She clearly isn't in the mood for this conversation.

'Have you been to Layla's parents yet?' I ask, chewing my gum nervously. Then I take Gorbachev out of the Kérastase pot and put him in my lap.

'Because you see, I found out it isn't Layla, but F'dila. I just caught her with her hocus-pocus, so I hope you didn't…'

Before I can finish my sentence, Baktha interrupts me. 'I went to Layla's parents yesterday. I kicked up a fuss there, if only you'd seen it! The entire neighborhood came to see what was happening.' Baktha is panting through the device, clearly pissed off.

'Oh.'

'And you're only telling me now?' she continues, 'You know, I talked to her father through the window, he didn't want to open the door… That poor, poor man. I called him an asshole and his daughter a whore!'

'Oh, no,' I sigh, and press my nails into my forehead. If only I *had* seen it. It sounds spectacular.

'What happened next?'

'At some point, there was a fire,' Baktha proceeds, 'so I left in a hurry, before they could accuse me of starting it.'

'What? I say, frowning. I put Gorbachev on my shoulder.

'Yes, that was pretty weird… Suddenly there was smoke coming out of the window and before I knew it everything was black. So the conversation abruptly came to an end. And now you're telling me this?'

'Alright, alright,' I don't really know what to say. I stretch out my hands, so Gorbachev can reach my fingers.

'Actually, I want to ask you something too, since you're calling,' Baktha says, the sound of suspicion in her voice.

'Oh, what's that?' Meanwhile I try to avoid thinking of any bit of Hatim and me fooling around. Would she have heard about it?

'Do you ever go to the club?' she asks skeptically.

'Me? Tssk… Of course not.'

'Oh, that's a shame. Because I would like to go to the club. But only the one Hatim always goes to.'

'What's your plan?' I ask, and throw Gorbachev on the mirror table a little too forcefully.

'Bust him. Wash him on a washboard in front of all his friends and wring him out like a sponge. That's my plan.'

'Good,' I say, 'in that case I might be able to arrange something.' If Baktha is planning to give Hatim a piece of her mind in the club, then of course I want to be there.

'When are we going?' Baktha says. She strikes while the iron is hot.

'Friday or Saturday, whenever you want,' I propose. Meanwhile Gorbachev is frantically attempting to crawl off my sweater, I stop him.

'Make it Friday. The sooner, the better.' Baktha says, determinedly. Hatim's wife is going to the club, that's bound to be a blast.

Surprised by the strange request I end the conversation and decide to message Layla to pick up the pieces and to bring her up to speed on the F'dila incident that happened at Lala Rosa… I lift Gorbachev from my shoulder and put him on the mirror table, then plop myself into the hairdresser's chair. What's taking Hatim so long? He should have been here ages ago.

'What happened?' Hatim yells from the doorstep. It's the first time I've seen him in a tracksuit. His faded sneakers fit right in with his outfit.

'He was probably still sleeping,' I hiss at Gorbachev.

Hatim barges in with heavy steps and walks towards me. Along the way he hoists his pants, which are way too big and sliding around, back up.

'Look what I found,' I say, eyes wide open.

'Where is she?' Hatim asks. To my astonishment he sounds worried. You have got to be kidding me...

'That hypocrite bitch is in the kitchen being pathetic with her crocodile tears.'

I get up, put Gorbachev on my shoulder and follow Hatim.

'What's the matter then?' Hatim asks. He starts to comfort that witch. F'dila, that bitch, she must have enchanted him!

'What are you doing?' I poke him in the back. Then I throw the voodoo doll on the kitchen counter. 'She wants to kill me and you're here comforting her! Are you out of your mind *ah*-idiot? Look! There are even pins in my eyes, do you hear me? That thing has been stabbed stiff with pins!'

'Be quiet,' Hatim orders me.

'Don't you think it's bad enough she harassed Dijana out of her job? Now what? Am I next?' I yell at Hatim, who's looking around sheepishly.

'What's the matter?' Hatim asks F'dila affectionately. Then he folds his arms around her. Baktha should have seen him like this.

'I don't know!' she sobs, and the dirty bitch swallows her fake tears, 'I was in the kitchen and all of a sudden she attacked me!'

'She was piercing pins into my eyes, look! There's even hair, *my* hair, in the doll! Check out those tufts!'

'Were you?' Hatim asks her, fully understanding. F'dila starts shaking her head.

'That's not my doll at all, I don't know where she gets this bullshit from. First she brings in a mouse and now it's a doll.'

'You dirty slut!' I want to attack F'dila, but Hatim jumps in between, so I thrust against his body.

'We'll leave *that* for later, babe,' he whispers into my ear unashamedly. The anger is raging and racing through my

veins… I fling Gorbachev on the counter and without thinking tear F'dila's apron off her body.

Everything spills out of her apron and rolls across the tiles of
Lala Rosa like Beardman's shells. Strange powders and amu-
lets…
   'Oh!' I cover my mouth with my hands. Her whole apron
was full of voodoo stuff, as if she's one of those street vendors
selling fake watches from underneath a big trench coat. So
this is how that apron was serving her secrets. It's just unbelievable! For a moment it remains dead quiet in the kitchen.
   It's as if Hatim has been flash frozen by a blizzard. The color
has drained from his face. His eyes remain tethered to F'dila's
collection lying on the floor.

All of a sudden, his eyes turn red, his face almost bursting
into flames. His hair appears to stand on end.

'You… filthy illegal!' Hatim, a slow mover, begins to shift.
'Get out of here! I never want to see you again!'
   Embarrassed, F'dila picks her torn apron up from the floor,
along with the supermarket scissors and all the voodoo stuff
that fell out of her apron's pockets.
   'Get lost you dirty witch!' Hatim is screaming over her head.

Phew, I realize we got rid of that witch, and I get the sense
today is going to end well after all.

'Hurry up, you stupid cow!' I take Gorbachev off the counter
to walk out of the kitchen. As I walk by, F'dila gives me a stare
that chills me to the bone.

All of a sudden, I feel a razor sharp cold in my neck. The snip is ringing in my ears… I turn around and see F'dila clasping the supermarket scissors with both hands. She's already holding a big tuft of hair in her hand. Like a demon she lets the locks glide out of her hands one by one… They whirl down like falling leaves….

I suddenly feel naked and vulnerable. In shock I stare at Hatim, who shakes his head and gasps for air, leaning against the kitchen counter. 'You women drive me crazy.'

I drop to the floor between my soft golden locks and pick them up.

'My beautiful, beautiful hair!' I cry.

—

CHAPTER 15

Layla

At a loss

Here I am, sitting on sheepskins again.

'Layla, *do* you or do you *not* want to get rid of Lala Rosa?' the sorcerer asks *again*.

'Ooh… I don't know.' I rub my neck fretfully. 'His wife was at our house yesterday,' my desperate words fill the room, 'thankfully the fire alarm went off. Everyone thought there was a fire and my father forgot about Hatim's wife. You should have seen him!'

'What, a fire?' The medicine man is clearly lost.

'Yeah, man. That's what I'm saying, his wife came to see my father yesterday,' I sigh.

'Baktha has visited your father?' He scratches underneath his hat as if something slowly begins to dawn on him, then strokes his shells with his fingers. This sorcerer is a genius, he even knows Hatim's wife is called Baktha.

'A total drama,' I continue, 'right at that moment I was using your bgor. That was the cause of the smoke. My room was literally black with smoke.'

'See, the bgor saved you from the situation,' he points out, 'your father got distracted and Baktha left. Then there were no more problems.' He does have a point.

'But what are we going to do now?' The blind man picks up

the shells from the concrete one by one.

'I really don't know.' I just don't know anymore; my sight is blurred by all sorts of problems.

The debt collectors, the secret of the salon, my thesis… Hatim.

'Then why are you here, sweetheart?' The medicine man starts rattling his cup.

'It's just, I don't know…. I want my lawyer's practice… And this Baktha woman suddenly showed up at our door… and… I just don't know anymore.'

'And the salon? Do you still want it in your name and to come clean about it? To share in the profit?' Even though I'm unable to see it, I could swear the man just winked at me from behind his aviators.

'Otherwise the business goes to Souad, or to Hatim's wife Baktha.' He keeps rattling his cup. 'Or even worse: F'dila.'

'What?' I look up. 'Souad? Baktha? F'dila? No way!'

'So?' without hesitation the medicine man throws out the shells again. 'Here, look,' he points at the scattered shells. 'His wife now wants to get her hands on the salon too. If you want, you can easily get rid of Lala Rosa. Exactly like you wanted. In fact, it will solve your problem instantly.' An awkward silence fills the room.

'I don't want to get rid of Lala Rosa. I certainly don't want to give it to his wife after everything she put me through!' I firmly fold my arms. 'Not to camel-butt Souad, either. She simply doesn't deserve it.'

'So, what's it gonna be?'

'In any case I want Hatim to myself, but I actually want it all,' I blurt out without thinking.

'Good, that's exactly what I wanted to hear,' the sorcerer says, as he picks up the shells from the floor and throws them out on the concrete once more. Then he picks them up again, shakes the cup with force, and scatters the shells back on the floor.

'There are many problems, my child.' He shakes his head.

'What is it? My studies? My lawyer's practice… Is there ever going to be one anyway?'

'No, it's Lala Rosa… Very, very serious problems.'

'Can I still fix them?' I ask desperately.

'Then I fear measures will have to be taken.'

What kind of measures? What is this man talking about?

'Souad and F'dila are still after Hatim, and now that his wife has her eye on the business too, you are basically surrounded by several enemies. They are like hyenas who have no difficulty eating you alive.'

'What am I to do?' I raise my shoulders helplessly.

'Come back on Friday, it is important you are here before sunrise. Then I will make sure you get everything.'

CHAPTER 16

F'dila

No mercy

The metal bench at the tram stop presses into my butt. It's freezing cold and the chill is penetrating each fiber of my body. Who ever thought it was a good idea to have people sit on the grate of a barbecue grill?

Nothing is left of the clear sky. Dark clouds are gathering. And then the locks of heaven open and heavy raindrops fall. They are cold and icy and I realize I didn't bring an umbrella. But I don't care anymore… Across the street, the doors of Lala Rosa are still closed. I put my clenched fists in the pockets of my apron and wonder what those two are up to. Would Souad get on her knees for Hatim too? Such humiliation, such disappointment!

I put my index finger in my mouth and supply it with a blob of saliva. I seal my oath by drawing a line on the window of the tram stop with my wet finger.

'They will never forget my revenge. I swear, or I shall no longer be F'dila.' An old lady sitting next to me, shoots me a suspicious glance, gets up and decides to wait for the tram further down the street. For the first time in years genuine tears are rolling down my cheeks. Thankfully I can see the light of the tram approaching. Soon I'll be out of here.

When I sit down on a deserted spot in the tram, I realize it's over… The salon that should have been mine. The man who belongs to me and who would make all my dreams come true. But this story does not end here in the rain. My revenge will be merciless, I promise.

I know he's there, but he won't answer. Determined as a fat louse in a rabbit's skin, I keep ringing the bell until he answers. 'Yes ?' his dark voice flows through the rickety intercom.

'Doctor, it's F'dila!' I blurt brazenly through the thing. Fortunately, the door opens immediately.

In contrast to my previous visits, the aisle and waiting room are empty this time. Except for the sorcerer, there is no human being to be seen. 'I don't usually see anyone at this time, but you just wouldn't stop ringing the bell,' the healer mutters as I follow him to his office. He sits down on his sheepskin and I take a seat across from him.

'Your powders and spells have done nothing! The voodoo doll hasn't worked!'

'You haven't paid me yet,' he grumbles.

'I would pay you in installments, remember!'

'Let's see,' the old man dismisses my comment. He starts to rattle loudly with his shells. I suddenly notice part of his beard has come loose. The skin that shows underneath looks smooth and even. Not at all like the grubby beard and the rest of his gray appearance. Fraud! It's all just a play that this swindler is putting on.

It took me over an hour to get here. I could have taken the subway; it would have gone much faster. Some decisions you cannot foresee the consequences of. Sometimes it's necessary to take different measures and not follow the usual route. I am not used to traveling by subway.

'But,' I suddenly hear the sorcerer cackle on, 'I'll make sure Lala Rosa will be yours again.'

'Never mind,' I say aloud, 'I have a better idea.' From the pockets of my apron, I fish the remains of Souad's voodoo doll: a pile of hay and a worn tiger print cloth that I picked up from the ground. And the fire letter, still intact. I throw them on the cold concrete next to the sheepskins. They land precisely on the cowrie shells..

Then I get up and quickly walk to the front door. Before I slam it shut, I yell: 'You filthy swindler! *Ah*-asshole, go and take your shit to the theater!'

I take the same route back by tram. I get off at the stop of Lala Rosa. I don't know what to do with myself. I clench my fists and stomp through the streets of Rotterdam Harbor. While the rain is pouring over me, I run as fast as I can, but I don't know where I'm running to… All I know is that I'm beaten. Hurt, deceived, broken. I am completely torn to pieces.

I feel humiliated and screwed, just like the day they called me a village witch. Not long after I decided to pack my things and leave for the big city to live with my aunt. Now it's as if history is repeating itself. Every time I am the one who is chased away. First from our village, then I was told to leave the Professors. And now this.

All hope is gone… The way Hatim called me a witch in front of Souad! And that healer, a swindler, promising me the world, but selling me a lie. I've been hurt to the bone. Everything is gone: my wedding, the Mercedes, the villa and the man who would pay for it all.

With white-knuckled fists I face the rain and the strong gusts of wind making several attempts to knock me over. But the wind will not succeed… My tears and snot blend with the rain. I fight and I fight against the wind, because I always fight… Until eventually I win.

Without fear I walk across the deserted industrial estate, where I am passed by cars, mercilessly splashing rainwater all over me. I don't care… Nothing hurts me anymore. I don't give a damn!

I stop briefly at the deserted industrial compound. I can no longer hold back my tears. A young Eastern European girl offers me a handkerchief. She is scantily clad and is hiding from the rain underneath a shelter. '*Ah*-girl, thank you,' I say to the young woman and take the handkerchief.

Further down the road is an illuminated hardware store. I walk over and go in to escape the cold and to shelter from the rain. The cold in my damp clothes is almost unbearable. I sniffle and shiver and actually want to call Boubker to pick me up, but instead I walk thoughtlessly past the shelves. Past all the tools and the countless pots of paint. I stop in front of a shelf with large jerry cans.

'Can I help you?' the blonde shop assistant asks. He spontaneously starts blushing when he sees the state I'm in. His hair stands up like a fan and the hairstyle reminds me of a poppy. Meanwhile, he stares indignantly at the drops of water running past my temples and dripping from my apron onto the tiles.

I continue my walk from Rotterdam-West to the Zoo. The headlights from passing cars blind me. I feel like a strange being in a world that is no longer mine. The rain keeps falling down like streaks of glitter in the deserted city. There isn't a living soul around.

Although I have walked briskly, I am overtaken by the evening. I'm drenched and cold to the bone. But I will persevere, because I am on a mission and I will execute my plans. You know what they say about a woman on a mission…

I get to a large roundabout with big coppery whale tails sticking out. Motorists whizzing past me like madmen. It's directly opposite Blijdorp Zoo, where Boubker and I went only last year. It was a beautiful and sunny day and I briefly go back to the moment… Meanwhile, I put my fists in the pockets of my wet apron and take my place in the queue at the gas station. In front of me is a Smart car and behind me a large black SUV is arriving, the type of car the people in my village would also be impressed by.

As soon as the young woman in the Smart gets ready to drive away, I walk to the pump with my Lowe's plastic bag. I realize I've never operated a pump. I also don't know what to choose. Leaded, unleaded or diesel? The Chevrolet behind me moves closer at a measured pace.

I don't know how to fill a jerry can with fuel either, so I just give it a try. First, I take the container from the large plastic bag and unscrew the thick cap. Then I lift the nozzle from the unleaded gas pump and press the lever. The jerry can fills up and not much later the pump stops.

The only other thing I need now is a lighter.

CHAPTER 17

Souad

The people at the club

'Come, give me that mouse,' Beardman says hastily. My fingers brush the short tufts of hair peeping out from under my red beret. I still can't believe F'dila cut my beautiful locks. I swallow my tears. Men love long hair…

For one split second I hesitate, holding Gorbachev in my hand. 'Beardman,' I say suspiciously, 'you're not going to butcher him, are you?' I don't trust this guy at all. What if he hurts Gorbachev?

'Give me that creature,' he says, sticking out his wrinkled hand towards me.

'Well, fine, alright then,' I say, reassured, and hand him Gorbachev.

'So this is a Russian mouse?' Beardman asks, holding the mouse in his lap, firmly stroking his fur. Gorbachev seems to enjoy it.

'Yes, a Russian mouse with a short tail.' Hamster, mouse… they're all the same. And the man is blind anyway.

'Not so convenient for jumping,' He giggles. 'Say, little mouse,' he continues, 'what's his name again?'

'Gorbachev,' I answer.

'Hello, little Gorbachev… Where did you get that name?'

'Oh, you know.' I know the name is Russian, but who exactly Gorbachev is, I don't really know. Could it be a Russian soccer player?

'Can you imagine, last time you wanted to butcher him!' I remind Beardman of the incident, 'in order to fight the witchcraft that wasn't even done by Layla but F'dila! If that was the case, Gorbachev, for no reason, would be -' oh, I can't bear to even think about it.

'Here.' He hands Gorbachev back to me. I put him on my shoulders and this time he stays there, quietly.

'What's next?' I ask the medicine man desperately.

'I will give you something for Hatim. Listen very carefully, because I shall say this only once.'

I listen to his words attentively. Somehow it feels as if I've only just now made progress. Soon the salon will be mine… Me, the owner of Lala Rosa. I won't need any of those men from the club anymore. From now on, I'll pay for my own drinks and win everyone's respect with heaps of shoes from Shoebaloo.

'Does Hatim drink?' Beardman asks me curiously. He's a fortune teller, right? Can't he just rattle his cup for an answer? See, sometimes I don't get him. He takes so long to get to the point.

'Of course he drinks,' I answer, annoyed. '*Wili*, who on this planet doesn't?'

'I mean, does he drink alcohol? You know; beer, gin, Bloody Mary?'

'Oh, yuck, I see, *alcohol*,' I say disapprovingly, 'he might, but I'm not sure.' Of course Hatim drinks. He acts like an actual drunk in the club.

'Good, because I am going to give you a powder. You should mix that with alcohol, otherwise it won't have any effect on him,' Beardman explains. From underneath his sheep skin, he pulls out a small square paper. It's a sort of mini-envelope.

'This powder has no side effects, right?' I ask to be on the safe side. Because you know what they say about alcohol and drugs. These aren't drugs, are they?

'No, because I'm only giving you a small portion. Mind you: too much of this powder can be dangerous. Hatim would start hallucinating,' the medicine man says. Then he hands me the paper envelope with the powder.

'So I should mix the powder with Hatim's alcoholic drink?' I ask and take the envelope.

'Yes,' he sighs.

'Okay.' I'm sure that can be arranged. Next Friday to be precise. In Club Tapis Rouge. I'll probably bump into Hatim there, like I always do.

'Not too much of the powder, you said?' I ask to be clear.

'Don't worry child, I'm only giving you a small portion, so nothing can go wrong,' he says reassuringly. Then he starts rattling his shells again.

As soon as I've put the powder into my bra, I walk out of the office with Gorbachev on my shoulder. The hall is crowded with women. They look up in surprise, one by one, both because of my French beret and my Russian hamster mouse. I couldn't care less and get my cell phone out of my skinny jeans to call Schmeegle, the well-off man I met the other day when I visited the School of Management. The man with the built-in navigation system in the windshield of his car.

What I need is classy transport to impress the people at the club. The car has to be big enough for Baktha to come along.

Baktha is coming, because I promised her. Think of me what you want, but one thing is sure: I always, and I mean always, keep my promises.

Schmeegle fits into this picture perfectly, 'right, Gorbachev?' I give my white Russian hamster mouse a loving kiss on its nose.

CHAPTER 18

Layla

The movie

It's as if everything is happening in slow motion. The sorcerer rattles his cup and the shells tumble all over the place. My life these days seems to consist of three things only: the hair salon, the trouble with Hatim and the sorcerer. Sometimes it's like watching a movie that is supposed to be my life: Layla the Movie. Phew, who in the world would go and see that.

Instead of praying early Friday morning prayers and asking for God's help, I'm here with a fortune teller. For convenience's sake we call such a sorcerer a healer. This is without a doubt a sin!

How did I end up lowering myself like this? I *have* to, because if I don't do anything, I'm screwed. In this situation, I have no other choice. Ugh, who doesn't say that when they're visiting a sorcerer? Us medicine man visitors, we all live a deceptive ready-made lie. The delusion of 'I have to because I have no other choice'.

'Are you paying attention?' the sorcerer wakes me out of my contemplation.

'Uh, what?' What is he talking about?

'This powder and that powder,' the sorcerer says, pulling

two paper envelopes from underneath his sheepskin. 'You must absolutely not get them mixed up! You would be asking for trouble.'

'No mixing?' I ask the man, a little confused. I have no idea what he is talking about. It's just like in college, when the professor is rambling and I'm browsing my book, while in fact I have no clue what he is on about and what page we're on – and to make things worse, I often have the wrong book in front of me too. In those cases there's only one option left: run through all the material at home, hoping to discover what the professor was talking about. After all he won't have been rambling for three hours for nothing.

'*This* powder is meant for Souad, F'dila and Baktha,' the medicine man emphasizes.

'I think we can take F'dila off the list, if you know what I mean.' I give the man a wink, he won't see it anyway.

'What do you mean?' he asks, his forehead suddenly covered in sweat. I have never seen him like this.

'You mean F'dila has disappeared?' his mouth is open wide. 'Yes, she was caught with a voodoo-doll... Go figure. Souad said it was meant for her, but if you ask me, it was me she was after.'

'Well, well,' the medicine man hesitates for a moment.

'Anyway,' he continues, 'this powder goes into Souad and Baktha's coffee or tea, for instance. Just to sideline them for a moment so you can get your 'work' for Hatim done.'

'What exactly does this stuff do?'

'It numbs them,' the old man says, 'they will be focused on themselves rather than you or Hatim.'

'Okay, that sounds good.'

'And this powder is for Hatim… But pay attention, you have to mix it with alcohol,' the medicine man explains.

'Alcohol?' I almost fall off my sheepskin in shock.

'Yes, that's exactly what I'm talking about: alcohol.'

'But I don't know if he drinks, I really don't.' He used to, but now… And how am I supposed to give him something with alcohol? I'm never there when he drinks. If I'm not mistaken, he only drinks when he goes to the club. How the hell am I supposed to go to a club when I've never visited one before? What do I tell my parents? I'm completely at a loss again.

'Yes, he does drink,' the sorcerer tells me and starts rattling his cup. Then he scatters his shells, 'look, it says here loud and clear: Hatim drinks alcohol.' I glance at the shells on the floor, but can't make a Bacardi or Spritzer out of it. The club is the kind of a place you don't want to be seen when you're a decent girl and an aspiring toga-wearing professional, right? Imagine if someone spots me there, recognizes me, and tells my parents…

'Alright,' I nod, and my brain starts working overtime. I doubt I can complete all those assignments. I've never met Baktha. I would have to hire someone and pay them to put the powder into her drink, but who?

'You will succeed,' the man suddenly tells me, 'today even.'

'Today?'

'Yes, look,' he points at the shells again, 'today.'

I race through the city on my bicycle to get to the salon on time.

Do I still love Hatim? I feel a knot in my stomach. My relationship with Hatim did bring me a lot. Two studies and a decent paycheck each month. *And* a lot of worries, because I still don't have a single document of the business. Plus there's the sneaky behavior around my parents and the lying to my colleagues.

Outside city hall, a white carriage and some dressed up ponies are waiting for the bride and groom. I hold still to watch the newlyweds coming out of the building. They take pictures with their family and witnesses in front of the stately doors. What an awful dress! I look a little closer and can't help but notice that the groom is significantly more attractive than the bride.

The ugly bride *does* have a man. A handsome man who is fully committed to her. I sigh, I don't even want to watch this anymore.

I wipe away my tears and let myself be distracted by the colored flags at a nearby fountain.

I open the doors to the salon, *my* salon. As soon as Hatim has downed the powder mixed with alcohol and handed me the paperwork of Lala Rosa, there'll be a lot of changes here. Why didn't I start this sooner? Why didn't I visit the medicine man before? Then the whole situation wouldn't have escalated as it has now.

I storm into the salon; I sure hope they didn't make a complete mess! Everyone, the customers *and* Souad, who's wearing some funny beret, is holding a foil package in their hands. Their mouths are stuffed. The place smells of stuffed *bara* with chicken, shrimps and hot sauce from Madame Jeanette. Would they have left something for me? I could go for a stuffed bara.

I barge loudly past the customers and into the kitchen. As I listen to the rustling of the foil and the ladies' whispering in the salon, I scratch my head a few times. In front of me is the huge pile of letters from the debt collector that I brought from home. Hatim had promised to take care of everything, the bastard! And look at this mess in the kitchen… To make things worse I lost one of my best hairdressers… It's not Hatim, the jerk, who lost a hairdresser: I did! It is my salon! My salon! Dijana is irreplaceable… Maybe I can persuade her to come back when the place is officially mine? She will come back when she gets a decent offer.

I walk back into the salon, where it is still smelling of *baras*.

'Who's next?' I ask grumpily.

'Must be the time of the month,' I hear the old lady in the green djellaba whisper. 'I think it's her thesis,' Souad says, winking at the old lady. I see how she sticks her gum underneath the hairdresser's chair.

'Ugh,' I sigh. Everywhere I look there are traces of cut hair and grease stains on the mirrors, as if someone put frying fat on them. And look at those tables! At Lala Rosa it looks like it does under my bed. One giant mess. They should call *Tabatha Takes Over*, except Lala Rosa doesn't have revenue issues. On the contrary, the customers would keep coming even if we would move into a cave.

'Could you stop sticking your gum under the furniture, please?' I yell at Souad. She looks at me weirdly and for the first time doesn't argue with me. 'There's a smudge of oil on your chin,' I add. She quickly walks towards the mirror, her nail file still clamped between her fingers. 'Can we please turn off the music, I have a headache!' I tell Tee, who's closest to the stereo.

'Who's next!' I bellow through the salon again.

'Me,' Souad suddenly says timidly. Her eyes fill up with tears and turn red. What is she talking about?

'Who's next? come on guys!' I yell impatiently at the waiting table. But it remains quiet. Then Souad pulls the silly beret from her head. 'Oh!' I exclaim, and cover my mouth with my hands.

There's silence.

'Would you do me first?' Souad breaks the silence.

'What happened?' I ask in shock, watching her from a distance.

'F'dila,' Souad says gloomily. Her fingers are clasping the red beret.

'If anyone can cut properly, it's Layla,' Green Djellaba says.

'Tee, turn the music back on, make it a banger, 'cause if my hair is coming off, it might as well be a party.' Souad sits up straight and looks at me trustingly. The ladies from the waiting table, Green Djellaba and Tee gather around us. I can't remember anyone ever visiting Lala Rosa with such short hair. The customers here never have short hair. They wear it long and extremely straight; or curly and in layers. At the very most a customer would go for a half long bob but that's the exception to the rule.

'I feel like a bride getting her make-up done with all her friends watching,' Souad giggles. I'm reaching for my Jaguar scissors on the table, but Souad grabs my hand. 'Wait,' she says. She pulls her own pair of scissors out of her tiger skinnies. 'Here, use mine.' Holding the small device I look at her damaged hair.

'I think we can make something out of this,' I tell myself and particularly Souad. The ladies around us keep watching attentively.

The music is turned back on and the vibe in the salon is

as it always is. Souad lets out a zaghrouta and sees herself to a fresh piece of gum. The smell of strawberries and sugar almost instantly fills the air.

I start at the back… I find it quite painful to make the first cut into Souad's golden, vandalized hair. That luscious head of hair, which she used to attract many men, is gone. It used to flow over her shoulders; now short is the only option. F'dila caused the most damage at the back. First Souad could only twerk like Miley Cyrus, now she's confined to the same hairdo too. I am determined to give Souad the perfect short haircut. You can say whatever you want about the Lala Rosa girls, but one thing is certain: they always look great.

When I get to the sides, I decide to keep them a little longer. I cut the hair at the top a little short into a cheerful crop. I shape the sideburns into wisps lining her face and keep her bangs long and casual: it goes well with the perky, feminine boys' cut.

I have to say: it turned out really well. 'Miley Cyrus will be jealous when she sees your pixie cut.'

Souad is almost unrecognizable. 'And, what do you think?' I ask, just before I start blow-drying.

'It looks really pretty on you,' Tee says, clapping her hands excitedly.

'What do you mean *pretty*,' Souad grumbles as she looks at herself in the mirror, 'I look like some feminist bitch.'

———

CHAPTER 19

Richard

Everything is okay

'Is everything to your liking, mister Smelink?' the driver asks as he opens the tinted window separating the driver's side from the limousine's private area.

From where I'm sitting in the limousine, the view across Rotterdam, the river, the bridges is, in one word, excellent. The limousine itself looks very good. Especially the white seats, the purple lights and the shiny champagne bar are impressive.

'Everything is okay, Cedric,' I tell the driver. 'Can I offer you something to drink as well?' I take a crystal glass from the bar. It has a purple napkin folded into it.

'On duty, sir.' Cedric grins.

'One Coke will do no harm, will it?' I suggest. 'And, please, don't call me "sir," I insist. You must never make a man in his midlife crisis feel old.'

'Well then, Richard, a Coke it is!'

After I've poured myself something strong on ice and handed Cedric a can of soda, I sit back down on the seat looking out across the city. Perhaps it's a good idea for Souad and me to sit together on the two-seater later.

'Are you attending a party tonight?' Cedric asks. I'm glad he's trying to make conversation. The limousines I sometimes hire to impress foreign clients are usually stark, scanty and significantly smaller than this one. Their drivers never really are good company.

'No, it's not a party, we're going to a cabaret club, a cultural comedy night… I think it will be a kind of theatrical performance.'

Especially for this occasion, I have put my best foot forward for Souad. I want to impress her even more than with my own striking car. When I showed it to her, she quickly wrapped herself around me and looked at me adoringly; with her tiger print outfit and her pink gum. I felt like a real man and I'd never felt that way before. So now I've arranged this beautiful limousine for her.

She surprised me when she called yesterday, asking if I would join her at the club in Brussels and if I would organize a limousine. 'I've never in my whole life been in a real limo before!' The naiveté in her, it makes me smile.

'Will the show be in French if it's in Brussels?' Cedric asks me.

'Ah, indeed, the language, I haven't really thought about that yet.' Oof, as long as they don't start speaking Arabic, because I don't know a thing about that language, but French should be fine. I take a sip of my cold drink and let the possibility of a show in an unintelligible language sink in for a moment. I certainly don't feel like watching a performance for an hour and a half if I'm not even able to follow it.

If it were up to *me,* we would be dining in Amsterdam at *Ciel Bleu* tonight, and order the six-course menu. I am certain Souad will appreciate 'Onno's Tasty Caviar'. The night would end in one of the Junior Suites at the Amstel Hotel, and tomorrow morning we would order an elaborate breakfast and go on a romantic canal tour. We might even visit the Rijksmuseum, where I haven't been for years. Would Souad have visited the Rijksmuseum before? Oh well, you can't go there often enough. The arts are never boring.

'If I'm not mistaken, we are almost there. Are you sure this is the address?'
  'Yes, very sure.'

Excited, I take a big sip from my glass and quickly glance at myself in the mirror. My hair looks alright and there are no hairs peeking out of my nose. Before I left home, I sprayed myself with just enough perfume and moisturized my face properly. If I may say so myself: I look like George Clooney.

———

CHAPTER 20

Souad

We'll make their heads spin

'That haircut looks really jiggy on you, Souad,' Layla says, fiddling with the lock of the salon door.

'Oof, I'm hot.' I use my jacket to fan myself a little. My armpits are filling up with sweat. 'You and your jiggy.'

'But I would hold off on the tiger print for now,' Layla continues, 'it doesn't suit your look anymore.'

'Here, let me do it.' I wrestle the key out of her fingers.

'No, give me that, I'll do it.' Layla takes back the key.

'No, let me,' I grab the key from her again and quickly lock the door.

'Can I get my key back?' Layla asks impatiently. Wow, what's with her?

'With a haircut like that I would wear more cool and business-like clothes,' Layla continues.

Maybe it *is* time I start dressing differently, particularly as I'm about to become the owner of Lala Rosa. I can picture it already: women's suits from Yves Saint Laurent and shoes from Jimmy Choo. Ah, the thought itself is divine: Souad the successful businesswoman.

'Man, it's freezing here,' I look around in surprise.

The streets around here are often chillingly empty in winter-time. That's weird, right? When the sun is shining, the streets in West Rotterdam fill up with the most expensive bling bling cars and crowds of people, but you never see them in winter. I've never understood where they come from all of a sudden.

I quickly put Gorbachev in the pocket of my jacket and pull out some gum from the back pocket of my skinnies. I notice my scissors are still in there.

'Well, see you later then,' Layla puts the key to Lala Rosa in her shoulder bag. The key to the business which will soon be mine. Then she gives me four modest kisses in a way that tells me she doesn't actually want to. 'On which side is your car parked?'

'Over there,' I say, pointing across the tram tracks.

'Alright, I'll walk up with you,'

'No need,' I tell her, 'Someone's picking me up in a minute.'

'Oh?'

'Yes, I'm going straight to the club.'

That Schmeegle should have been here already, what's keeping him? He will show up, right? Otherwise I'll smash his navigation windshield next time I see him.

'To the club?' Layla's nose is reddening from the cold.

'Yes, to the club. You know I go to the club every once in a while. Or are you going to give me an attitude all of a sudden?' I look at her defiantly. I'm really not in the mood for this kind of crap. Layla always preaches that decent girls don't go to the club.

I accidentally press Gorbachev, who has snuggled up in my pocket, a little too forcefully. He immediately starts squeaking. That bitch better not give me an attitude or pick a fight with me now. Seriously, I'll smack the next person giving me an attitude right in the face. I can no longer control myself.

That trick F'dila pulled me has turned me into a furious volcano on the verge of bursting… That's how I feel. I wipe away a tear before anyone sees it.

'No, I… it's where Hatim always goes, right?' Layla's eyebrows look like two merging bridges.

'Yes, he's usually there.' I blow my nose into a paper towel, which I accidentally put in the pocket where Gorbachev is.

'And do you see him there then?'

'I ignore the crackerhead, of course. What do you think?'

'Can I come?'

'You want to come to the club? Uh, sure, you can join… What are you going to tell your parents?'

'I'll think of something,' Layla sighs. Her glassy eyes are suddenly shimmering in the pale shine of the lamppost. Everything looks prettier in the dark. Sometimes it only takes a little light to make everything shine. It's the same in the club. Everything shines and shimmers in the dark, even though you don't see a thing. And that's for the better, really.

What's going on with this chick, anyway? It's like she's trying to hide something. What is she afraid of… Can I trust Layla or not? If I have to believe Beardman, I can't.

I don't want to trust her, but I have enough enemies. Part of me doesn't want Layla as a potential enemy, but I know deep inside that you can't trust anyone in this world. Not even your best friend. Still, taking her to the club will do no harm.

'When are we leaving, then?' Layla asks, impatiently checking her watch.

'Take a chill pill, we're getting a ride,' I say. If there's one thing that annoys me it's people constantly looking at the time like total stress cases. The ones who never take the lead and keep knocking on your door to know exactly what time things start and when they end. And I find it particularly annoying when it's about a carefree night at the club.

'Who's giving us a ride? It's not Hatim, is it?' Layla seems about to burst.

'Of course not, what do you think? Schmeegle is taking us.'

'Uh, Schmeegle?'

'You know, the guy with the built-in navigation system in his windshield. I met him at the School of Management.'

'*Ah-Wili* Souad! You've got to be kidding me!' Layla punches me on the shoulder.

'I'm not,' I giggle girlishly. Doesn't the bitch know already? I can get any man I want. I decide not to mention the fact that Hatim's wife Baktha is joining too for now. What do I care, I'll just act as if I know nothing. I'll just pay attention to the powder the medicine man gave me and focus on a happy ending.

The limousine turns into the shopping street.

'This is the bomb, girl! This is how we'll make an entrance at the club!'

Layla doesn't know what to say other than '*Wili, wili!*'

'*Wili,* what? Simply *boom*: stretch limo. I swear, we'll make all the heads spin at *Tapis Rouge*!'

CHAPTER 21

Richard

Whiskey and Coke

Why did Souad bring a friend? Why did she bring that hamster on her lap? I thought we would be spending the evening with just the two of us.

So much for my plans for the Junior Suite at the Amstel Hotel. 'Cheers.' I symbolically raise my glass of sparkling water. I would much rather drink something else, but tonight, in the company of Souad and her friend from work, I'll just stick to non-alcoholic beverages.

'Wow, this is so much fun!' Souad is sipping her pink energy drink and from time to time cuddles the creature in her lap. I have to admit it does look somewhat endearing.

'Would you like me to get you a glass?' I ask with my most charming smile.

'No, a can is fine,' she tells me somewhat curtly.

'Wow, this really is a beautiful car. I would love to go traveling in one of those,' Layla looks around in utter amazement. Then she quickly returns to her iPhone.

'Really fun.' Souad puts her arm in mine. I don't know where she left her hamster and I honestly don't care… I look at her moon-shaped face. Gosh, what has she done to her hair? She looks barely sixteen with her hair this short. Especially wearing those tiger print clothes. My friends at the tennis club should see me like this!

Then suddenly Souad presses her soft, glossy lips on my cheek and gives me a big kiss. Who knows, this evening might end in the Junior Suite of the Amstel Hotel after all.

'I'm glad you're enjoying yourself,' I tell her, trying to sound mysterious.

'Oh, driver, stop! Can you roll your window down?' Souad suddenly pulls her arm away from mine and throws her can of soda on the table.

'Cedric, she has something to say.' The window slowly rolls down.

'We need to pick up another person!' Souad yells through the music.

'Oh?' Cedric mumbles. Who are we picking up?

'Who are we picking up *ah*-girl?' Layla puts her iPhone aside.

'Baktha, we need to pick up Baktha.'

'Baktha, ugh.' Layla sighs.

'Yo, take it easy,' Souad says, as she takes her drink back from the table.

'You can't be serious…' Layla continues.

'Yes, I am. I told you just now, so what are you nagging me about?'

'Asking Baktha to come along! Have you lost it?' Layla passionately taps her forehead.

Souad simply looks the other way and plays with her hamster. She yells at Cedric commanding him to stop at the right house.

Who is this Baktha they keep talking about? Instead of asking, I decide to pour myself a whiskey after all: it looks like it's going to be a long night. The limousine stops in front of a house where the curtains have been drawn shut.

'Schmeegle darling, I just want to thank you for this amazing car, seriously, it's totally awesome! Seriously, respect. You are a real jiggy-man, if you know what I mean.' Souad snuggles up a little closer to me.

'Is that so?' I carefully sip my whiskey. I am a jiggy-man. That must be a compliment. 'Well, to a nice, jiggy evening.' I raise my glass, which I've almost emptied already.

In a way, I find it quite exciting… Who is Baktha? Perhaps she's an incredibly beautiful woman?

Then Cedric's arm appears, and, attached to it, completely unexpectedly, a stout woman wearing a hijab. What on earth?

Layla and Souad look at each other uncomfortably. Did I just see Layla snap at Souad?

The woman is wearing some sort of long-sleeved medieval dress, covering her from head to toe and a thick poncho on top. She has trouble getting into the limousine. Souad did not just pick up her mother, did she?

People at work should see me now… My friends at the tennis club should see me now! I look like a joke with this woman!

Before the woman enters, she lifts her sort of long dress and says something incomprehensible in Arabic. Then she makes a face at the bar. 'Tsk, Tsk, alcohol.'

'Sorry,' I utter, panicking, and quickly turn the bottles, so that the labels are no longer visible. As if that makes any difference.

The woman, who seems to have trouble walking, sits down on the first available seat next to the door.

'Oof,' she sighs. She stares ahead as if we are invisible, as if she is taking a ride on an ordinary local bus. Next thing you know, she will pull out her public transport card.

'What a disaster.' The woman suddenly stretches out her hand in my direction. 'I haven't even introduced myself.' She slides toward me. What am I supposed to say to her? That I am on a date with her daughter? To my surprise, the woman speaks Dutch fluently and looks significantly younger up close than she did from a distance. Confused, I extend my hand to her, unsure if that's allowed in their culture. Hopefully I won't get into trouble with her husband or her brothers, or a scooter gang. You quite often hear about those sorts of things.

'Can I pour you something to drink?' I ask the woman. 'A Coke maybe?' Baktha takes her seat and looks around a little anxiously.

'Yes, that would be nice.'

CHAPTER 22

Baktha

Blonde sluts

The Dutch man presses the Coke into my hands. I'm so impressed I can't even think straight anymore. I quickly sit down on my seat at the window and tensely take a sip from my drink. Never in my whole life have I been in a limousine, my neighbor friends should see me like this! My husband Hatim does have a fancy car, but I hardly ever sit in it. I always walk and when it rains, I take the tram.

'What a disaster.' I rub my cheek with my fist. 'Sorry Souad.' I turn around to greet her. Then I greet her friend too, and say '*Salaam,* my name is Baktha.' The girl turns pale as she hears my name and says 'hello, I'm Layla, Souad's colleague.'

'Layla?!' I say a little too loudly and quickly sit straight again. What a disaster, what a disaster… Isn't this *the* Layla? Whose father I visited a few days ago to call him an asshole? *What a disaster!* It's the Layla I called a whore!

The Layla who was supposed to be having an affair with my husband Hatim, which in hindsight turned out to be a misunderstanding. Now Hatim is said to be having an affair with some F'dila, who according to Souad is here illegally, but *does* have the salon put in her name. 'Is that even possible?' I asked Souad over the phone. 'These days anything is possible, with the internet and all.' Souad had told me. Then I asked my neighbor, but she didn't know either. I would like to ask this Dutch man, surely he knows, but I don't dare. Anyway, Layla is here and I decide to just ignore the whole incident. That's how you solve problems effectively: by simply ignoring them. Eventually everything will fade into oblivion. Besides, I have other things to focus on tonight, such as the powders the blind medicine man has given me. One of them should be stirred into the drinks of the ladies and the other into Hatim's alcoholic beverage. And then we'll see who's boss around here!

I put my hands into the pockets of my djellaba, where I'm keeping the two envelopes. I drew a big cross on the envelope that's meant for the ladies of the salon, so there's no confusion.

'It's just to keep them out of the way, so that you can do what's needed,' the sorcerer explained to me. That's exactly my plan, to get these two chicks out of the way, so I can do what's needed. According to the medicine man they also have their eyes on Lala Rosa *and* Hatim. Those blonde sluts, I'll show them.

While Layla is playing with her phone, Souad is openly flirting with the Dutch guy whose name I have forgotten. She should be ashamed of herself… Would she behave this crassly around Hatim too?

The view across the river is truly beautiful, I rarely get here by car these days. Before we had children, Hatim and I would often go for a ride, and drink coffee along the highway. We also went on holiday to the south of Spain once. I remember us dining in intimate restaurants every night. But once we had children, everything changed. Hatim no longer saw me as his lover, but as 'the mother of my children'. Maybe he's confusing me with his own mother? Since then he stopped paying attention to me and I surround myself with the various neighbor women. They are all facing the same problem, so they interfere with my issues claiming they are experts on the subject. As if they all know better… As if all they have are good intentions. I'm not buying it.

I drink the last bit of Coke and put my hand in my pocket to check on the envelopes. It's haram, I know, but I have to. I have no choice…

'Would anyone like another drink?' I ask. I must and I will get the salon into my hands, and when that's settled, I'll throw Hatim out the door. Screw him!

Their responses follow quickly: 'I'll have a Coke!' 'Well, I could go for a whiskey and Coke.' Ugh, him and his whiskey! But so be it… 'Layla, would you like something to drink too? Layla?'

'Uh, I'll have a…'

'Coke too?'

'Fine.'

CHAPTER 23

Layla

Should I call a doctor?

Why is Baktha here? I don't understand! I'll just ignore her, pretend she isn't here. Pretend I'm not here. Pretend I've never dated her husband and pretend the incident, her visiting my father, never happened. She called my father an asshole and me a whore, but I'll pretend I don't know about that. We just won't discuss it, we'll pretend nothing ever happened. It will soon blow over. There are two ways to deal with your problems: one is to stick your head in the sand. The other is to visit the local medicine man.

I doubt if Baktha even realizes who I am. There is a chance she knows… What is she even doing here and why is she coming to the club? And why did Souad invite her in the first place? Seriously, I don't trust this situation one bit. As soon as I run into Hatim in the club, I'll mix the stuff into his drink and if I have to, I'll take the first available train back to the Netherlands. I've got a feeling this night is going to turn into one gigantic mess.

I close my phone and take a sip from my Coke, which tastes a little weird. Bored, I gaze outside. Souad is giggling away with that Richard Smelink and her guinea pig thing. She isn't taking the creature to the club, right? I feel Baktha's eyes poking into my back like sharp chisels. Oof, if looks could kill…

At least the limo is *da bomb*, with the crystal glasses, the velvet and all kinds of fancy light effects. The vibe however is anything but great. Suddenly I feel nauseous and dizzy.

'I feel really, really sick,' Souad says.

'Me too man, I feel awful,' I say, but I don't want to think about nausea… One more bump or turn and I'll throw out everything that's in my body, right in the middle of Richard Smelink's fancy limousine. So I just gaze at a fixed point in the distance, hoping I won't have to be sick.

'What did you girls eat?' Smelink asks uncomfortably.

'Do you want me to open a window?' the driver asks, but it's already too late…

Souad quickly grabs the champagne bucket from the bar and throws out all the ice cubes. They scatter in front of our feet, just like the shells the sorcerer throws out of his rattle. Souad hurls into the bucket with a range of vomiting sounds. The pungent smell of warm, acidic vomit fills the limousine in no time.

'Pull over!' Smelink tells the driver, who stops the limo alongside the guard rail. We all get out of the car as fast as we can. As soon as the driver has secured her guinea pig, Souad climbs over the guard rail and disappears behind the bushes, where she almost forces out her intestines.

My stomach suddenly and unexpectedly shoots out of my throat and I accidentally puke against the shiny rims of the car. The heavy vomiting session just won't stop, I feel pressure building up behind my eyes and it seems to last forever. Even when there's nothing left to throw up, my stomach just won't stop. Exhausted, dizzy and out of breath, I wipe my mouth with the tissue the driver hands me.

'Here, have some water,' he says, after which I start vomiting even more.

'What did you girls eat… Should I call a doctor?' I hear Smelink say.

'Are you alright sweetie?' Baktha rubs my back with her warm hands. She seems unfazed by the entire incident.

We stop at the nearest gas station so we can freshen up in the toilet.

'Jeez, this is embarrassing.' Souad combs her short hair back in place. 'Throwing up in the champagne bucket, that's one thing I'll never forget.' I burst into laughter.

'That poor man, he must think we're crazy,' Souad says, as she dabs her face with cold water.

We drive through several tunnels with strange side roads and pass many traffic lights. After the driver took two wrong exits, we finally arrive in the center of Brussels.

Everyone in the limousine is focused on themselves. Souad is frantically chewing her gum while staring outside, Baktha has interlaced her fingers and Smelink is gazing at the ice cube floating in his glass. The limousine comes to a halt.

'We're here.' Souad suddenly says. She presses her nose against the window attentively. I quickly wriggle my fingers into my pockets to check the envelopes are still there. The powder I'm supposed to mix with Hatim's drink and the one that is meant for Souad and Baktha. The sorcerer was right about me visiting the club and running into Baktha today; his predictions came true. But I'm still not sure if I'll do what he told me…

The driver opens the door courteously and we get out of the car one by one.

'Well Madame Club, where do we go?' Smelink asks Souad. Then he starts giggling, I don't know why.

'This way,' Souad calls, but after a few yards she stops walking. 'Actually no, it was the other way.'

'Where is it then?' I ask impatiently.

'Are you sure it's here?' Smelink remarks.

'Wait a sec guys, I can't think like this! Yes, this is it.' We walk a few yards into the street until we arrive at a big door. It seems to be locked and there is no sign of any life. The door is firmly shut. On the red banner above the door, I read the elegant letters:

Club Tapis Rouge

Souad knocks on the door a few times, 'hello, hello.' She tries several times, then she checks her watch. 'Oh, I think we're a little early,' she remarks carefully.

'What do you mean?' I ask suspiciously. 'What exactly do you mean by early?'

'Well, you see, at the moment it's 9 pm.'

'What time do they open then?' Baktha asks, now also a little impatient.

'Around midnight, one-ish.'

'What? Couldn't you have told us earlier?' I give her a firm push.

'Nine, ten, eleven, twelve…' Souad counts the hours on her fingers.

'What a disaster, what a disaster! What do we do now?' Baktha rubs her cheek with her fist.

'I thought I'd be home by eleven.'

CHAPTER 24

Souad

Club Tapis Rouge

'No!' the bouncer, who looks like the hulk and speaks with a heavy Flemish accent, refuses to let Baktha enter the club. '*Allez,* you are not allowed in like this!'

'What do you mean?' Schmeegle asks, running his hands through his hair, all worked up. In my entire life I've never met a man with highlights. Schmeegle is the first. I picture him at the hairdresser's, his hair wrapped in tin foil; what a turn off.

'We want to go in, what *is* this?' Schmeegle says.

'I'm sorry sir, but I think I've made myself very clear: I cannot allow women in hijabs and people wearing Nike Air Max to enter.'

'Refusal of admittance, you can't be serious!' Schmeegle says, astonished. Suddenly I find him quite attractive and manly, macho even… If I ever decide to start wearing a hijab, I can rest assured Schmeegle will accept me just the way I am and treat me respectfully. Now that's what I call a real guy!

As befits me, bad-ass Cleopatra, all dressed up in my tiger print leggings, high heels and see-through blouse, I decide to have my say too: 'You bald crackerhead, your head's too heavy for your own neck to carry!'

'Madam, would you not address me in such a provocative tone, please?'

'I'll decide for myself how I speak, okay? Turning against your own people like that, ugh!'

'Madam, we have rules here and everyone must stick to those.'

'Ugh, get lost with your rules! Are you with the populist party or what, not allowing hijabs into this place? Right-wing extremist perhaps? Your mother wears a hijab *ah*-head!'

'Let's keep my mother out of it, alright? Besides, my mother would never visit a club.' The bouncer quickly gives me a disapproving look.

'What, you have a problem with it? I myself am quite curious what your boss is going to think of this.'

'Madam, I am not allowed to let women wearing hijabs in, and the same goes for people wearing Nike Air Max.'

'*Ah*-shut up, with your security jacket… Go protect something important, instead of refusing access to hijab-wearing women. What's wrong with a hijab? What the hell is wrong with a hijab? Can't she have a good time or what? Can't she participate in things other people have a right to enjoy?' I am screaming at this point.

'Madam, we have rules here. You are not allowed in like this.'

'*Ah*-fuck you and your rules! What kind of rules are those, what kind… You can't even explain them yourself! I am allowed to wear a dress that just about covers my butt crack, but I can't come in wearing a hijab. I am allowed to look like a slut, but not like a devout Muslim? *Ah*-fuck off *ah*-crackerhead making five euros an hour to stand next to a door,' I keep screaming. Meanwhile, I gesture to Baktha to go in anyway.

As soon as she disappears into the club, I pull Schmeegle along by the sleeve of his jacket. The fabric feels fine and soft. '*Ah*-forget the crackerhead, let's go inside.' Layla has quickly followed Baktha in.

'You see that limousine over there?' I point out to the bouncer.

'Yes madam, I can see it quite clearly.'

'Park it for us, will you?' I tell him contemptuously. Then I turn to the driver. 'If you just give him the keys, he'll park our limo for us.' Now the bouncer really looks at me as if I'm crazy and shakes his head. The driver gets into the car and parks it next to the club.

I turn around, pump up my boobs and swing my hips. I take a big gulp of air and hold Schmeegle firmly by the arm, 'come on.' Usually I arrive here all by myself and at the end of the night I leave with a lot of cash, a man and his fancy car. But today is different.

We walk towards the entrance of the club. First we cross the deserted lounge with the red carpet. Then we walk through a thick cloud of shisha-smoke leaking out of the decadent hall. It's so dark in here, you can hardly see a thing. Where would Baktha be? And where's Layla? I can't see them anywhere. I can only see strange eyes reflecting the lights.

'Shall we sit here?' Schmeegle suggests. He points at a square table with a red paper cloth and a kitsch tissue box on top.

'Here? Are you crazy? This is where the losers always sit!' I bluntly point out the boys around me.

'Maybe we can sit over there,' I gesture towards the well-lit area further on. That space is separated from the dark section by a big wooden wall with holes. You can barely see through it.

'Oh, there's another area?' Schmeegle looks around confused.

'Yes, *that's* the VIP lounge. *That's* where we're supposed to sit.'

We walk towards the dance floor. The disco colors are coming right at us and there's a small band playing all kinds of wedding tracks. It's the same kind of music we play at Lala Rosa. It just sounds a whole lot better when it's performed live in the club. The singer, a dwarf with a beautiful voice, always wears custom made shoes of crocodile leather. He has been singing here for as long as I can remember.

Schmeegle stares at the little person in surprise. 'Stop staring, he doesn't like that,' I whisper in his ear.

'Oh, right, of course.' Schmeegle says, staring his eyes out. 'Well, I feel like dancing,' I say.

'Are you good at belly dancing?' Schmeegle asks awkwardly.

'Belly dancing? What do you mean belly dancing?' I punch him on the shoulder. 'I think you mean shaking my hips. I can shake it, like a blender.' No matter how dark it is, Schmeegle cannot hide the red spots in his neck.

'So, this is the club?' Schmeegle asks shyly. I take his hand and lead him further into the VIP lounge.

'I believe there won't be much comedy and theater,' he mentions giggly.

'Comedy? Theater?' I look at him in surprise, what is this guy talking about?

'*Bonjour,* would you like a VIP table or would you prefer a seat in the back?' the owner of the club asks us. He seems to have entirely forgotten about our little incident. I wonder if Rasheed is here tonight. I browse the tables with dressed up men sitting in their tailor-made suits, wearing expensive watches. I look at the ladies at their tables with their revealing outfits. Rasheed is nowhere to be seen.

'How is it different from a regular table?' Schmeegle asks the owner.

'Regular tables are in the back,' the man points at the dark area, where there's mostly *shisha*-smoking steam heads. 'Drinks over there are 20 euros each. And here,' the owner indicates the VIP lounge, 'you'll get a table for 200 euros.'

'What, that much?' Schmeegle says indignantly. *Wili, wili,* this guy is stingy! I hope we won't sit down in the back, because then I'll dump him right away. I'm not going to sit among the losers.

'But you will get a tray with drinks and unlimited refills,' the owner continues.

'What kind of drinks?' Schmeegle asks. Oof, I hate this kind of shit! Why doesn't he just take a table? We drove all the way here in a friggin limousine, and here he is, trying to cut costs over a VIP table! I want to run my fingers through my lengthy locks like I always do, but that's impossible with this short crop. Ugh, ugh, triple ugh!

'Anything! Anything you want…' the owner explains invitingly. 'Champagne, Black Label and Red label, any kind of liquor.'

'Oh, I thought you wouldn't be serving alcohol,' Schmeegle turns to me excitedly.

'Well, if it's going to take this long there won't be any drinking at all,' I say impatiently.

'You are absolutely right darling – we'll have a VIP table,' Schmeegle says resolutely as he points towards the VIP area. I follow the owner to the table with Schmeegle at my side. We're seated close to the singing dwarf, with a good view across the dance floor. I can't see Baktha and Layla. Oh well, I need them like a hole in the head.

As we're about to sit down on the red velvet bench at the round table, Hatim comes walking into the club. He's with a couple of friends and walks straight towards a free VIP table. He hasn't seen me… I wonder if Baktha saw him coming in? This will be fun.

'It's just a club.' Schmeegle is tapping his fingers on the table. 'It's just a nightclub. This isn't a theatre, is it?' He's talking to himself as he looks around in surprise.

The waitress looks like a beer barrel wrapped in a red dress from the bargain store. She walks towards us carrying a large platter, in the middle of which fireworks are sparkling.

'Well, well,' Schmeegle continues. I've noticed he can't keep his eyes off the ladies on the VIP benches. They are all wearing daring dresses and of course they are covered in heaps of make-up. Their real Chanel bags are on the table. They might be clad in silk and scarlet, but an ape's still an ape if you ask me. Apparently, men take a different stance.

'Hey!' I poke Schmeegle in the ribs. 'You're drooling all over the place! Do you want me to get you a room?'

'Oh, that won't be necessary, sorry about that,' he dismisses jokingly. Then he opens the bottle of champagne. The pop is sadly drowned out by the music. He pours two glasses. One for himself and one for me.

I sip my champagne while keeping a close watch on Hatim. The crackerhead seems to be having a great time with his friends and a couple of hired prostitutes. I wonder when Baktha is going to make her move, but first I have to get the powder into his drink. I hope her revenge won't beat me to it.

Hatim and his buddies are drinking, laughing and bellowing about. They haven't got a clue.

'Come here,' I beckon the waitress in the tight red dress to come closer. She instantly walks towards me. Then she bends over in a seductive pose. 'Would you like to make a quick 50 euros?' I whisper in her ear. The woman nods and waits. I pull out my envelope containing the powder. 'I want you to mix this into a glass of hard liquor and hand it to Hatim. You know who he is, right?' I look at the woman and wait. I sure hope she won't rat me out to that crackerhead, 'cause then I'm dead.

'Of course I know Hatim,' the waitress smiles, pretending we're making pleasant conversation. 'But it's going to be quite difficult.' The woman suddenly has an attitude.

'Alright, I suppose 100 euros will do?'

'You got it.' The waitress quickly pulls the envelope out of my fingers.

CHAPTER 25

Layla

Powders for Hatim

Baktha is sitting a few tables further, hiding behind the huge drinks menu. Although we are seated close to each other, I pretend not to see her. She's doing the same.

'What would you like to drink?' the waitress asks. She looks like a red sausage and her hair's done up like a banana.

'I'll have a Coke.' It hasn't even been two seconds before the woman tosses a can of Coke with a black straw on the table.

'Pay up,' she says.

'Can I do that later?' I ask her. If I'm not mistaken, I just saw Hatim walking in with some friends and, I'm not surprised, a couple of bitches. They look like first-rate sluts. Asshole… Fortunately I can just about see them from here.

'No, you're paying now.' The woman impatiently clicks her heels on the parquet.

'Okay, relax,' I tell her, and quickly open my wallet. 'How much?'

'Twenty euros.'

'What? Twenty euros for a Coke?'

'Yes, all the drinks here are twenty euros. It's more expensive in the VIP lounge. A platter over there costs two hundred euros, so what are you whining about?'

I put the blue note on the table with a heavy heart.

'Thank you.' The waitress smiles at me and grabs the money off the table. I take a very careful sip from my drink and since it cost me twenty euros, I'm going to take all night to finish it. Just like they do at the teahouse. Some people there take so long to finish their coffee or tea, they have it warmed up by the waiter later in the afternoon. It is kind of like a teahouse in here, except with a lot of liquor and peroxide women with Chanel bags.

Two young guys next to me are smoking *shisha*. Meanwhile they stare at the dance floor, where there are mostly women dancing with each other. Gosh, and I thought Souad had the biggest hips. Her air cushions are nothing compared to what you see on the dance floor: ladies dressed in revealing skinny jeans and tight dresses. What am I supposed to do with that powder for Hatim?

'Everything alright here?' the waitress asks as she walks by again.

'Oh, sure.'

'Don't you feel like dancing? You're so alone out here,' she asks me nicely.

'Oh, I'm fine over here,' I tell her.

'You're pretty,' the woman continues, 'if you go dancing, you'll stand out and probably be invited to a VIP table by a businessman. Then you won't have to pay for your own drinks anymore.' The woman winks at me.

I want to tell her: I can pay for my own drinks, thank you very much! But the woman has just given me a wonderful idea.

'Say,' I ask her, 'would you do something for me?'

'What?' The woman bends over curiously.

'See that man over there? I really like him.'

'Which one?'

'That one over there, at the table all the way in the back, among his friends, the one in the white shirt with the high collar.'

'Oh, that one.' The waitress starts giggling. 'You want me to put something in his drink?'

The woman is getting very close now and I can smell her armpits. We look each other straight in the eye. 'For a hundred euros I'll make sure your stuff ends up in Hatim's drink.'

'What? A hundred euros?'

'Take it or leave it.' The waitress rises and walks away from my table.

'Wait, wait, wait a sec!' I yell and quickly search through my bag. I put all the money I have in my wallet on the table. 'Fifty, twenty, that's two, and that makes three… Seventy-three euros and ninety-five cents, that's all I have.'

The waitress takes all the money off the table, including the small change. 'Give me the stuff.' I pull both envelopes out of my pocket, one for Hatim and one for Souad and Baktha. But which one was meant for Hatim?

'Hurry, hurry! I don't have all night, what if someone sees us?' The waitress is impatiently tapping the table. Which one was it, I really don't know… What do I do?

'It's now or never,' the waitress says. She bangs her hand on the table and gets ready to walk away.

'Wait, wait a sec,' I tell her again. What to do? 'Here, it's this one,' I hand her the envelope in my left hand. 'No, take this one.'

'What is all this?' the woman sighs. 'Do you even know what you want with these envelopes?'

'You know what, here. Just put them both in.'

'In the same glass? They're both for him?'
'Yes, just put both powders in his glass.'

'Whatever you want.' The woman shrugs and disappears with my powders.

Oof, what a relief. My shoulders drop, as if a big burden has been lifted off. As soon as Hatim drinks the powders, all my worries will vanish.

Look at her sitting there. Baktha, a human heap gone stale… I can't believe *she's* his wife. All of a sudden, I'm completely over Hatim.

Contently, I take a big sip of my Coke and make myself comfortable. Let the games begin!

CHAPTER 26

Baktha

Money squandering

What a disaster… Out of habit, I forcefully rub my cheeks with my fists until they feel hot. They've probably become red, making it seem as if someone has beaten me. But here in the dark behind the drinks menu, no one will notice anyway.

What a disaster, these aren't just so-called apostates. What a disaster, these aren't some Dutched-down immigrants with great jobs and a great position in society who suddenly start drinking wine. These could have been my barely educated neighbor friends! The kind of women who wear a djellaba by day, and apparently parade in the club at night, full glass of champagne in hand. Ugh, I spit on them!

I watch all the women in their fancy clothes. They look like sluts. Those men, all married, skimping on every penny at home only to spend it all on these bitches here. What have I done to deserve this? My husband, the snake, is also here, and probably not for the first time.

I stare at all the young boys sucking *shisha*, ogling the dancing girls. Those chicks have crawled onto the dance floor only to entertain the men around here! And my husband, the asshole, is sitting happily among them.

I'm boiling with rage, I swear… I'm boiling inside. I would like nothing better but to stand up and throw that platter off his table and smash those liquor bottles on his head one by one. I could barely hold it together when those three *whores* sat down next to him. Hatim even put his arm around one of them!

I swear, I'll make a cinnamon roll out of him! Just watch it *ah*-head! You just sit here and enjoy yourself, while you always leave me and the children at home by ourselves. I have to be the mother *and* father, you piece of shit, you tin-head! Just wait and see *ah*-Hatim, I'll make kebabs out of you!'

'How did you get in here?' the waitress asks me indignantly.

'Shht!' I tell her. The woman is wearing a bright red dress, which fits as tightly as a Speedo. Some airheads think they are supermodels, like Bella Hadid, and that they can wear just anything. I would love to hand her my poncho, but instead I say: 'Girl, come a little closer.' The waitress bends over and comes dangerously close… Wow, she could use some deodorant, oof.

'Would you like to make two hundred euros?' I ask the woman, giving her a big fat wink. I throw the money on the table right away, because money takes care of everything. The woman raises her sharply epilated eyebrows and presses her red nail into the stack of notes. 'All you have to do is put this into the drink of that man in the VIP lounge,' I tell her, and show her the small envelope. 'The guy over there, in the white shirt.'

'You mean Hatim.'

'Exactly, yes.' My husband, which slut doesn't know him? All these sluts know him better than his own children do!

'He may not notice anything and it has to be mixed into his glass of *alcohol*, you understand?' The waitress carefully takes the money and the powder off the table. 'Madam, almost everything here is alcohol.'

'You know what, I'll give you two hundred and fifty, just because you're so sweet. But don't tell anybody!' I pull out another fifty euro note. Hatim is not the only one who can squander money. I took this money out of our shared bank account, and usually I'm very careful spending it. I'm saving for a house, a new car, our children's education, and I'm just saving for the sake of saving. How could I know he is spending all our money on whores and liquor? From now on, everything will be different, and his lazy, irresponsible life will be over when this evening ends.

'No worries,' the waitress says, 'this powder too will be mixed into his drink.'

CHAPTER 27

Richard

Who is the bearded man?

I am well on my way into a delirium, and I've lost count…
How many double Black Labels did I down already? Oh well,
it doesn't matter… Who would have thought? Here I am at
a cultural club, and instead of watching a comedy show, I'm
looking at sexy dressed up girls swaying across the dance
floor. They all have great hips and shoulders and loose hair
like wild tigers. I glance at Souad's boyish pixie cut. She's en-
thusiastically chewing her gum. Why did she cut her beautiful long hair? She now comes across as a little too integrated
and assimilated; tough and not very charming. I let the last
sip of whiskey glide over my tongue.

The overall mood here is truly enjoyable. My friends should
see me like this: they would be dead jealous. Look at all those
exciting exotic beauties. It's a real shame Souad got rid of her
long locks. I stroke her soft pixie cut with my fingers.

'Will you come and dance, Schmeegle?' Souad asks, blowing
a pink bubble with her gum.

'Oh, gosh…' I utter. Then all of a sudden, the singing dwarf
is standing at our table. He's singing an enjoyable song and
in the meantime whispers something in Souad's ear. Souad
whispers something back in return. What are they talking

about? Then the singer, with his shoes of crocodile leather, walks over to me.

'In honor of Schmeegle!' he yells through his microphone.

'He called your name,' Souad whispers in my ear.

'Yes, I heard.' I raise my glass out of politeness, 'cheers.'

'You don't understand, he called your name,' Souad says earnestly.

'In honor of mister Schmeegle!'

'I don't understand…'

'If the singer calls your name, you have been chosen. Then you get to request a song and then you *must* pay him.' Souad says, a little agitated now.

'How much, then?' I take a sip from my drink.

'Five hundred euros.'

'What? That much?'

'Do you want to give him a ten euro note in front of all these men? Do you even know how much they pay for a song? You can't just hand him some change when they all pay a Grand or two!'

'A what?'

'A Grand, a thousand euros, and some guys even pay two. It's considered a real failure when you don't pay enough for a request.'

I top up my glass with Coke and ice; the whiskey suddenly becomes hard to swallow. I search the pockets of my jacket with my free hand, looking for my wallet. 'I'm not paying five hundred euros for a song,' I say while handing the singer a fifty euro note.

'In honor of Schmeegle!' the singer continues, he clearly has no trouble accepting the money. The man shows no intention of leaving. 'In honor of Schmeegle!' he repeats through his microphone. I surrender and throw another two fifties on the table.

'Now you get to pick a song,' Souad says contently. 'Great move,' she continues, 'to throw the notes on the table one by one, that way it really seems as if you paid a lot.'

'What?'

'You get to choose a song,' Souad says, wrapping her arm around me. The singer keeps standing impatiently at the table and fills the room with sounds I don't understand.

'Which song?'

'I don't know, just a nice song.'

'Eric Clapton?'

'Are you crazy? Does he look like he can sing Eric Clapton?'

'Alright,' I tell the singer, 'make it Aïcha.'

The song seems to work, everyone in the VIP lounge is singing along sentimentally, and Souad gets to sing a bit of the chorus. She sings extremely out of tune. Perhaps she should stick to shaking her endless hips in the future.

An hour goes by and it seems to get busier by the minute: too busy for the owner to keep up. Some of the VIP guests are standing by the wooden wall, impatiently waiting for a table. The dance floor is so crowded that all you can see are the squirming sides of people and whirling hips of women. Heels and stilettos are hopping to and fro. The singer is making good money, because he keeps calling the 'name' of some VIP guest, who in turn throws a stack of bills on the table. I do hope he doesn't come to our table again.

They pay serious amounts, especially compared to my hundred fifty-euro tip. Where do these men make that kind of money?

Souad is having a great time on the dance floor, and she does just what she said earlier: 'I'll dance out those bitches one by one.' Whoever dances close to her, is in for a sweep from her sturdy hips. Around her there's a spacious circle: all eyes are on Souad.

I refill my glass with ice from the bucket and mix some rum with Coke. There seems to be some commotion a little further on where it's dark and gray with smoke. The unrest increases after a few minutes. I can't exactly see what is happening from here, but it seems to be serious. Even the VIP guests are now turning around on their fancy sofas to see what's going on in the darker, less luxurious area. The singer gets distracted too, he stops singing in the middle of a song, while hitting a high note. He sounds awful and the microphone screeches... What in heaven's name is happening back there?

I look around and start searching for an emergency exit, in case something dangerous happens. But I find none! The kitchen is right behind the bar, so there must be an exit there. I keep a close watch on the darker area. Where is Souad, actually?

The turmoil only gets louder. The owner walks to the back and all the girls stop dancing. The dance floor is slowly emptying, the live band stops playing... except for the flashy 80's lighting there's no festivity left on the dance floor. What is going on and where has Souad gone?

'Schmeegle?' Souad wipes the sweat off her forehead. Without explaining she pulls me up by the hand. 'Come, quickly.'
    'What happened?' I follow Souad through the dark, the rum and coke still in my hand. Careful not to waste it, I quickly down it and place my glass next to a *shisha* setup on one of the tables we pass.
    We walk past the cloakroom and into the cold outside. A

little further on I see Cedric, he's leaning against the car and looks up. A crowd of people hurries out of the club, as if there is a fire.

'Look!' Souad points to the roof of the club.

'My God, there's a man on the roof, he's going to kill himself!' I hear someone shout. The man takes off his clothes, roars, bellows and gurgles. He yells: 'All of you are trying to make me crazy!'

The man throws his pants, which he just took off, towards the astonished crowd.

'Gosh, shouldn't we call the authorities?' I reach for my phone. 'What if he jumps off the roof!'

'No!' Baktha yells. She's suddenly standing next to us and agitatedly pulls the phone out of my hands.

'Well, who do you think...' I utter, but I'm too distracted by the man, who now starts scattering money... It's raining banknotes and the crowd is not ashamed to pick them all up. Then the man yells: 'Do you want more or less money? '

'*Ah*-head, get down. You're out of your mind!' The owner of the club snaps furiously at the hysterical man on the roof.

I take a deep breath, 'this might end really badly.'

'It's Hatim, Baktha's husband,' Souad whispers in my ear. For the first time she's not chewing her gum, for the first time I can see the fine lines in her face... She's beautiful.

I look at the women from a distance and realize I ended up at a theatre show after all. Or it's the whiskey and I'm drunk...

Souad: '*Wili, wili,* what if he takes off his underpants? I really can't watch this.'

Layla: 'What should we do?'

Baktha: 'Nothing at all.'

Layla: 'But what if he jumps off the roof?'

Baktha: '*C'est la vie.*'

Souad: '*C'est la merde, you mean.*'

Baktha: 'What a disaster, he took off everything! What if they take him away in an ambulance and they check his blood! We need to think, that's what we should do: think.'

Layla: 'How can you still think? *Ah*-head, your husband is about to jump off the roof, naked! *Ah*-don't you understand *ah*-head?!'

Baktha: 'Shut up, before they suspect us… What a disaster… We did nothing wrong, right?'

Souad: 'I agree with Baktha, before you know it, the police come, an ambulance, the whole shebang. Before you know it, they suspect us of 'weird' stuff, if you know what I mean.'

Layla: 'We've gone too far. We should…'

Baktha: '*Ah*-shut up you, for the millionth time! We should, we should… We shouldn't do anything! Please do us all a fa-vor and take your whining into the limousine.'

Souad: 'Layla is right, we should do something…'

Baktha: 'Are you starting now too? *He's* the one who wanted to come to the club. *He* wanted to drink alcohol with his sluts. Well, as far as I'm concerned, *he* can go to hell on that roof.'

I walk towards the ladies and decide to get involved. 'Your husband has completely lost it,' I tell Baktha. 'We should really call an ambulance now… don't you understand?' Everywhere I look I see hysterical men and women picking up banknotes from the ground. In the background there's Cedric, already opening the doors of the limousine. Perhaps we should just leave?

'No! We shouldn't do anything! We just have to think about this calmly.' Baktha briskly wraps her poncho around her shoulders.

Layla is tightly clasping her phone. Finally, someone who has come to her senses. But instead of calling someone herself, she answers her phone. She turns her back to the incident and doesn't look at Hatim on the roof. She pretends there is nothing going on!

'*Wili,* I'm dead! I swear, I should never have listened to that Beardman,' Souad says, hitting herself on the head.
    '*I'm* dead, you mean!' Baktha starts.
    'Who's the bearded man?' I ask. I am completely at a loss.
    '*Ah*-shut up, I can't hear a thing of what's being said!' Layla is waving her hands. She runs towards the limousine, her phone pressed to her ear, trying to get as far away from the noise as possible.
    The two women next to me are looking around sheepishly. Are they really planning on doing nothing?

Layla suddenly walks back to us, clasping her phone in her neck. 'Something terrible happened, we have to get to Lala Rosa.' Her eyes fill up with tears.

'What are we supposed to do with that dickhead over there then?' Baktha points at the roof.

'Just take him with us, before they call the police,' Layla says, shaking her head impatiently.

'I'll go get him,' Souad says, 'I'll fold him up and carry him down on my back if I have to.'

'Darling, please be careful.'

F'dila

My Mercedes and my villa

Red tongues of fire fan out from the windows of the top floor. The entire building is ablaze. A large crowd of spectators is gathering in the street. They have rushed here on their slippers, some even in bathrobes. Why are people always drawn to fire?

The couple from the second floor is propped up on the sidewalk by neighbors, who have fled their homes too. An old woman with a flowerpot hairstyle is resting her arms on a walker while her elderly husband is acting like a small child searching for his mother. I feel his pain, because my heart is breaking too…

The police arrive first, followed by the fire brigade. The street fills up with people waking up from their sleep. As if the fire is calling them all.

I wipe the gasoline from my fingers on my wet apron, the soles of my shoes are soaked with cold rainwater. I am shivering and sniffing from the cold and yet I stay. I have thrown the jerry can into the nearest waste container. Large, dark clouds of smoke curl out of the building. Everything smells of synthetic materials and burnt hair tortured by a blazing hair dryer.

I close my eyes and listen to the sound of the crackling fire, ringing in my ears like a pleasant melody… Like the sound of dry autumn leaves in the forest. It rains shards of glass when, one by one, the windows burst. The fire truck siren drowns out the noise of the crowd and the flames. A strong gust of wind is blowing dark autumn leaves from bare birch trees across the paving stones and over my shoes.

There are intertwined fire hoses everywhere. Firefighters are running around, trying to put out the flames. The police are cordoning off part of the street with police tape and ask the crowd to take a few steps back. The ribbon says: Do Not Enter.

They will never suspect me… Who would suspect an oppressed little woman? One with two headscarves and an apron? In their eyes I am nothing more than a silly cow. The subordinate, the stateless, the worthless. That is the place they have reserved especially for me and there will never be another one. They are just as single-minded as those fools back in my village were.

I can feel the heat even at this distance, even though I'm hiding all the way in the back of the staring crowd. They are completely unaware… Here I am, the spectator of my own play.

'No! No!' The screams cut through the chilling silence in my head.

A large car parks alongside the fire trucks, it's a limousine. The kind of car I could deeply impress the people in my village with, those bastards who would always call me… I cry iron tears of clotted blood – for my wedding, my Mercedes and my villa that will never come, will never be there. My sweet dream, my young girl's desire to escape a shabby life. My hope for a better life, a beautiful life. The humiliation and my revenge.

I watch Lala Rosa melt into the sea of flames, I see my hometown vanish in the sea of flames, it is all swallowed up by the fire. You can say and think whatever you want… But nobody will ever call me a village witch again.

—

A few months after the fire Layla finished her studies. Baktha, of all people, helped her get all the information she needed to fully claim Lala Rosa. The insurance company reimbursed Layla for the fire damage.

With the insurance money the two women started a new hair and beauty salon in Rotterdam West. The place is very stylish and they can barely handle the constant flow of customers. Layla managed to convince Dijana to come back. She has her own work space where all day long she does nothing but epilate women as she listens to their problems. There is a cozy coffee corner where Tee and Green Djellaba have a permanent seat.

Souad too decided to open her own business. 'Leopard Shoe' is of course covered in leopard and tiger print. Each customer leaves the store with a pack of Bubblicious. It is hard work, but with Gorbachev on her shoulder Souad finally got the independence she always desired.

The night Lala Rosa went up in flames, Hatim did not come home. 'Don't you ever show your face here again!' Baktha told him. He has since been spotted at a powerful medicine man... One who is said to be able to turn water into ice. Hatim is most certainly plotting his revenge...

'*Aah*-F'dila! Have you completely lost it?', Boubker roars from behind the wheel. 'You're totally right, honey,' I tell Boubker, making him feel as if he's in charge. In reality, it's me at the helm. I have always been at the helm. He is just my puppet.

Since the Lala Rosa incident, I have realized I have to be a bit more careful with Boubker, that crackerhead. Ultimately, he was the only chance I had to get a residence permit. And he isn't all that bad, really.

'Alright, you have it your way!' Boubker says, hitting the brakes hard. The abrupt halt almost makes me throw up. I put my hand on my belly and feel my unborn child kicking…

I get out and take a seat behind the wheel. 'Now what do I do?' I ask Boubker. I have never driven a car in my life, I don't even know where to start… Then again, how hard can it be?

'*Ah*-never mind, just let go… Yes! I'm releasing the handbrake, yes! The car will just roll into the village by itself,' Boubker says.

With me sitting behind the wheel, we very slowly roll down the bumpy dusty road into my village. We pass the first houses and it's not long before a puddle of children races out and starts running along with the car. The main thing is that it seems as if I'm driving the car… It's not an S-class one, but it *is* a Mercedes.

For a moment I glance at Boubker… Not the man I had in mind, but he is a man… and there is a wedding coming.

Contently, I stroke my blouse, with my pregnant belly showing.

I sigh deeply as Boubker pulls the handbrake. The car grinds to a halt. Finally the time has come. Finally I'll show all those

village fools how successful I've become, because now everything is different…

There's always gonna be another mountain
I'm always gonna wanna make it move
Always gonna be an uphill battle
Sometimes I'm gonna have to lose
Ain't about how fast I get there
Ain't about what's waiting on the other side
It's the climb

The struggles I'm facing
The chances I'm taking
Sometimes might knock me down, but
No, I'm not breaking

Miley Cyrus, 'The Climb' (2009)

Ah-head	'*Ah*' is used as a stopgap, to indicate exaggeration
Bara	A Surinamese snack
Bgor	Incense
Burqa	Garment that covers the face
Djellaba	Authentic Moroccan coat
Ghassoul	Mineral clay from the Atlas Mountains
Hammam	Bathing establishment
Haram	A sin, forbidden
Hijab	Religious veil
Sabon el beldi	A natural soap made of olive pits
Wili	Derived from an Arabic word, used to indicate something is unpleasant
Zaghrouta	A high-pitched vocal sound representing joy, accompanied by rapid movements of the tongue

ACKNOWLEDGMENTS

Without you this would not have been possible. Thank you from the bottom of my heart Mani Nordine, Umar & Sylvia Elba.

Rotterdam Mayor Aboutaleb, Adil Khayat, Karim El Guennouni & Tirza Oudheusden, Irving Vorster, Marianne van den Anker, OPEN Rotterdam, Safaa Khelifati, Nassira Boudhan, Rabiaa Bouhalhoul, Chafina Bendahman, Friso Smits, Bilal Aznou & Yvette Heutink, Hind Laroussi, Moufid Sbai, Adnane Bennis, Dewi Reijs & In-Soo Radstake and Virginia Bird. Thank you for your unwavering support.

Thanks also to the staff at Cafe Zurich, Amsterdam.

A very special thank you Joni, Isa, Michiel, Winne, Geeti, Leigh, Mark, Trish, Earl, Mohammed, Jamila, Loubna, Ikram, Danyal Zayn, Amira, Lina, Adriana, Cris, Sharon and my partner in crime Josh.

'The parents' culture, the dreams the girls
have and also the image Dutch society has of
Moroccans, that's what *El weswes* is about.'
Elle

'In short, *El weswes* is about something substantial.
It is a fast paced, well written novel.'
Trouw

'Najoua shows that individuals can be different
in their thinking and acting while sharing basic
feelings, fear of rejection and the desire to be loved.
This book is certainly not for the youth only.'
Generation Now